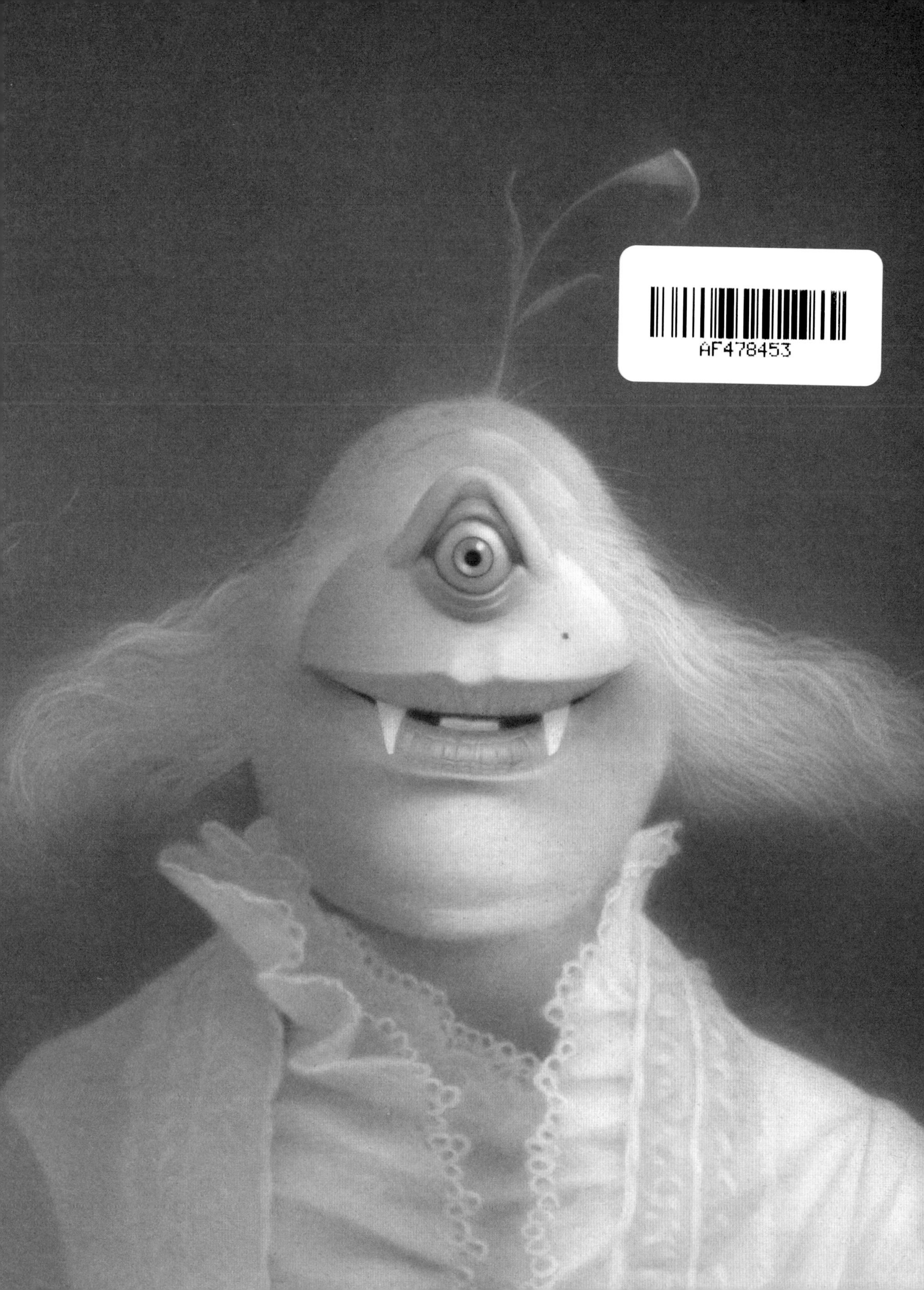
AF478453

TRAVIS LOUIE'S
CURIOSITIES

Travis Louie's

CURIOSITIES

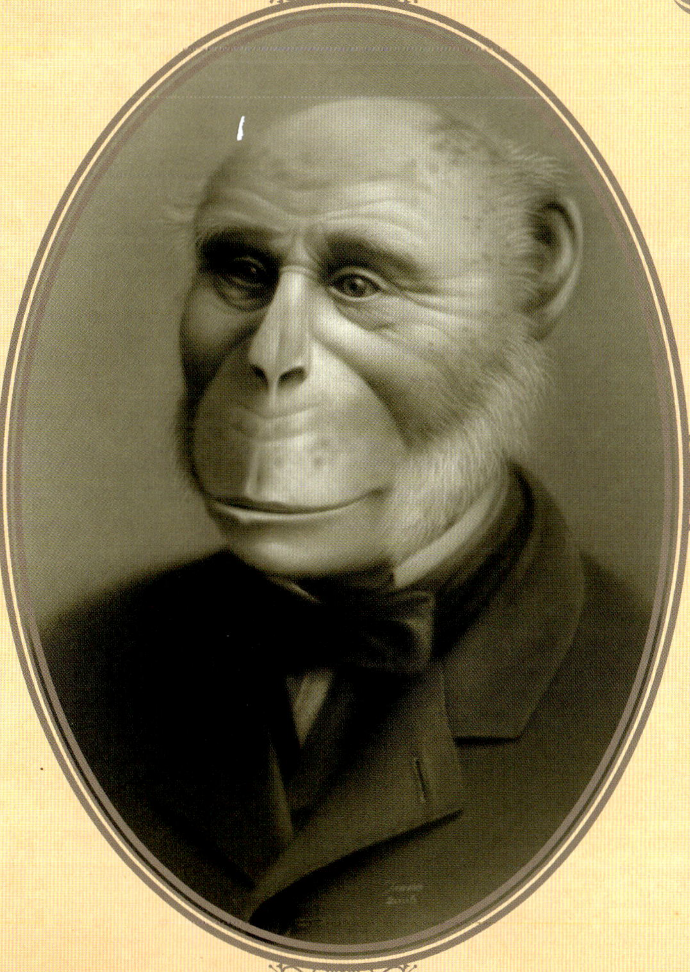

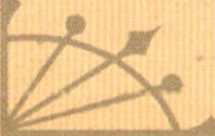

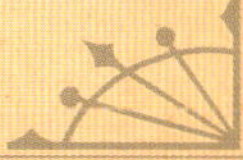

BABY TATTOO BOOKS® • GALLERY 1988
LOS ANGELES

Baby Tattoo bids a fond farewell to Alan Cunningham
Friend, Photographer, Teller of Curious Stories
1936 - 2009

ISBN: 978-0-9793307-5-9

This book was printed with five collectible covers.

Design by Laurie Young

10 9 8 7 6 5 4 3 2

Published by
Baby Tattoo Books®
Los Angeles
www.babytattoo.com

Gallery 1988
7020 Melrose Avenue
Los Angeles, CA 90038
www.gallery1988.com

Manufactured in China
Fabriqué en Chine

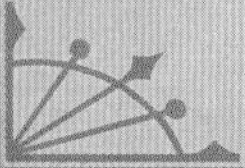

A Portrait of the Artist as a Young Monster

Travis Louie's monster portraiture showcases a finely wrought world of sympathetic grotesqueries. Chimerical creatures are stuffed convincingly into formal suits and elegant dresses, with pleasant (if sometimes somewhat befuddled) expressions on their lumpy, whiskered, and multi-eyed faces. Clawed hands hold elegant canes, or rest gently on fine leather chairs. Feminine fanged lips are outlined with carefully applied lipstick. Tufts of cotton candy hair swirl upward like ghosts engaged in a cemetery waltz. Pop-eyed cyclopean subjects sit patiently for the photographer's flash, and dog-faced dandies wear their finest Edwardian suits and pocket watches, posing as regally as bank presidents. Travis has created a menagerie of dignified portraits painted in daguerreotype tones and ensconced in ornate vintage frames. His works of art seem stolen off the walls of an opulent yet decrepit haunted mansion.

The Who's Who of this genteel ghoul gallery is depicted in formal and rigid Victorian poses and is rendered in meticulously tight black and white acrylics and graphite. The images are so masterfully painted that they look more like turn-of-the-19th century photographs than paintings created with a brush, with surfaces so smooth and brushstroke-free that some viewers are sure the work is digitally created even when told otherwise. The exquisitely moody lighting in the paintings, which evoke the spirit of a bygone era, is influenced by German Expressionist films and film noir fantasies, as well as by the hazy, stark tones of Civil War tintypes.

Coupled with his astonishing painting virtuosity, Travis's singular vision is tempered with a healthy dose of un-self-conscious humor and imaginative storytelling. Each "character" (a term appropriate to multiple definitions of the word) comes complete with a written biography detailing his or her peculiarities, perversions, and peccadilloes. In fact, the lives of these imaginary ancestors start out as random thoughts, story fragments, and scribbles in Travis's ever-present notebook. Over time, the various personalities are expanded upon until their faces spring fully formed onto the silver screen in Travis's mind, ready finally to make their visual debut.

Travis Louie himself is a bit of an interesting character, born in Queens, New York, to Chinese parents. He wears his hair in a waist length black braid, sports a heavy, no-nonsense New York accent, and speaks Cantonese. He married his wife Diana when they were both going to art school, and they have a sprightly young daughter and a houseful of creepy crawlies they call pets.

Taking care to steer clear of any professional "dramas," Travis has become the go-to guy for artists and dealers when navigating the murky world of art relationships and proprieties. He has a reserved demeanor that occasionally splits open to reveal a love for nerdy sci-fi and fantasy, an encyclopedic knowledge of art history, and a goofy wit. Having refined his art skills for decades, he is now to the point where he spends most of his time ceaselessly painting in his basement art studio to fill the incessant demands of a long list of notable art galleries and a legion of fans. Travis's work seems to resonate with an impressive array of collectors who react with surprising passion and keen acceptance to even his most bizarre and gruesome (but kindly) beasts. Partially this attraction is from the sheer eye delight that results when looking at a painting by Travis Louie, or from the journey of discovery that occurs when reading one of his wild stories; but there is another connection as well . . . a kinship viewers share with these awkward, most unlikely of beings.

For who hasn't looked in the mirror and sometimes felt like a misfit —a misunderstood and ungainly creature just trying to get along, trying to find others like themselves, and trying to exist (as much as possible in a monstrous world) in a state of grace?

— KIRSTEN ANDERSON
April 2009

For Diana and Elizabeth

IN 1867, GORDON THURSTON SMITH WAS BORN WITH SIX EYES. LIKE OTHER
children who had more than two eyes, he was ridiculed and teased. For most
of his childhood he hid away in his room, dreaming of binocular vision.

He had many siblings. There were fourteen brothers and sisters who
all lived on the upper floors of a very large house. Gordon lived in the
basement and stayed there until his six eyes became highly fashionable,
and his anger at the outside world had subsided to a level of "extreme
indifference."

By the time he decided to emerge from the cellar and experience the
outside world, his brothers and sisters had all grown up and married. He
now had many nieces and nephews who loved their "Uncle Six Eyes." They
marveled at his ability to move all six of his eyes in different directions at
once. They wished they had six eyes, instead of the "boring" single eye they
each had on their shiny, bald heads . . . just like their parents.

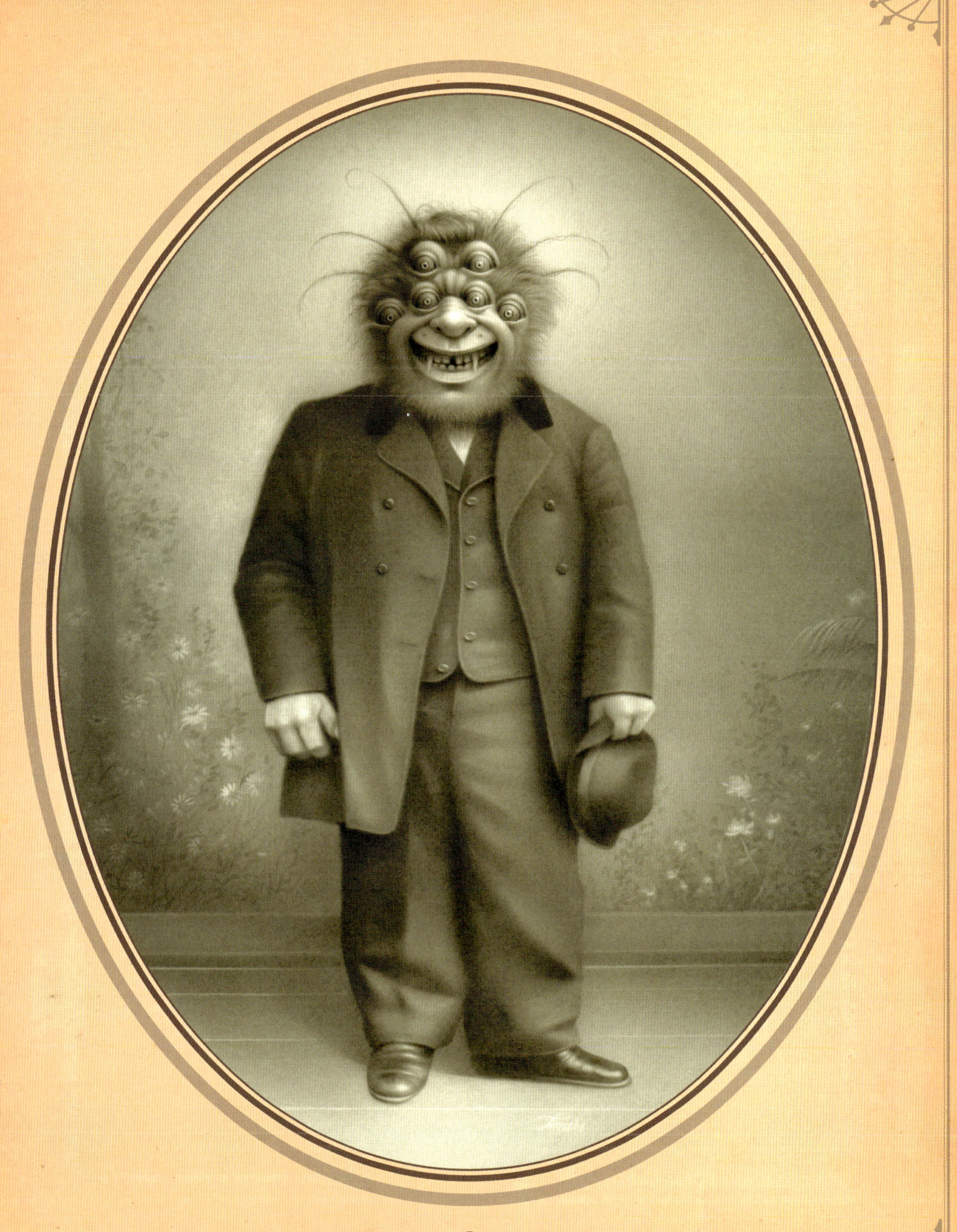

➤ Uncle Six Eyes ➤

THOMAS WORTH WAS AN ANGRY MAN WHO DEVELOPED A HABIT OF KICKING things when he lost his temper, which was quite often. He managed to kick most of the people in his town for one reason or another. As a result, he was always alone and became unemployable. The townspeople often wondered why he was so angry all the time. Some said he was kicked by a mule when he was a child. Others said his mildly insane father would dress up like a clown and give him regular tauntings until he was strong enough to taunt back. Regardless of his origins, he terrorized his town in a constant fit of rage and intolerance.

One day while eating an apple, he bit down hard with a rotten tooth. The pain shot through him quickly and his temper flared up as usual. He turned and saw a goat grazing in a nearby field. He rushed over to it and kicked it. Incredibly, the goat stood up on its hind legs and shouted, "Nasty-boy, I'll make your face just like mine!" The sight of the goat frightened him and he fainted. He woke up feeling dazed and confused a few hours later. As he lifted himself up and staggered drunkenly toward home, he wondered if he had passed out from the pain caused by the bad tooth and if that unsavory apple had given him the bad dream with the goat. As he reached the center of town, he noticed everyone was staring at him strangely and wasn't sure what to make of it. It made him angry, nonetheless, and when he tried to kick one of the gawkers, he stumbled on a rock and almost fell face-first into a puddle. As he righted himself, he caught a glimpse of his reflection in the water. A curious thing had happened . . . somehow the goat's curse from the "dream" had come true.

From that day on, he did his best to stave off his previously unmanageable temper, in the hope that his appearance might change back. He was nice to everyone, especially goats. He remained "goat-faced" until the day he met his demise. He was kicked to death by some angry, "clown-faced" reindeer.

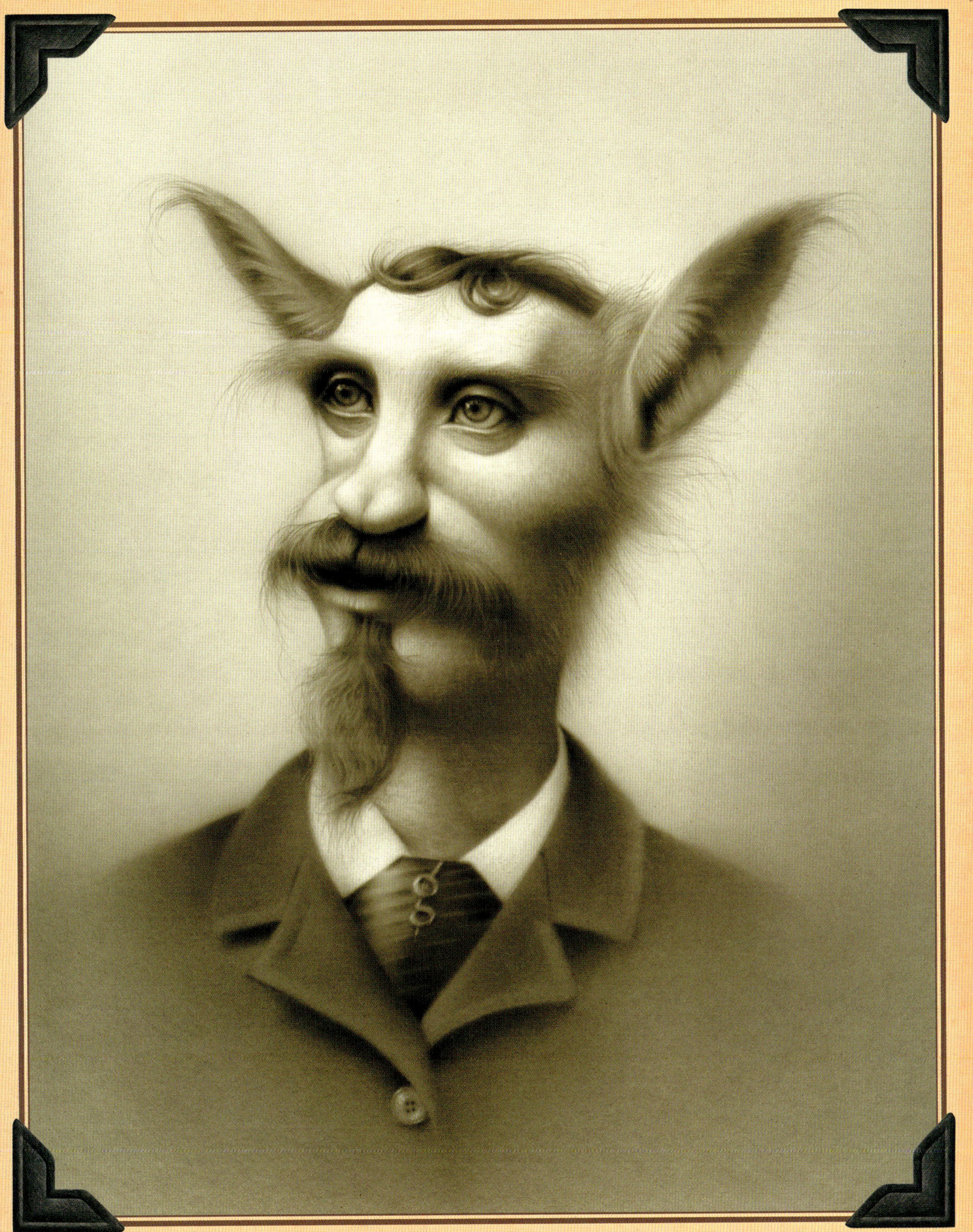

CURSE OF THE GOAT

SARAH FITZGERALD LIVED IN A SMALL HOUSE IN WALES WITH HER PET FISH, EMMETT. He was mostly snapper and part lung fish. She treated him like a small dog and carried him wherever she went.

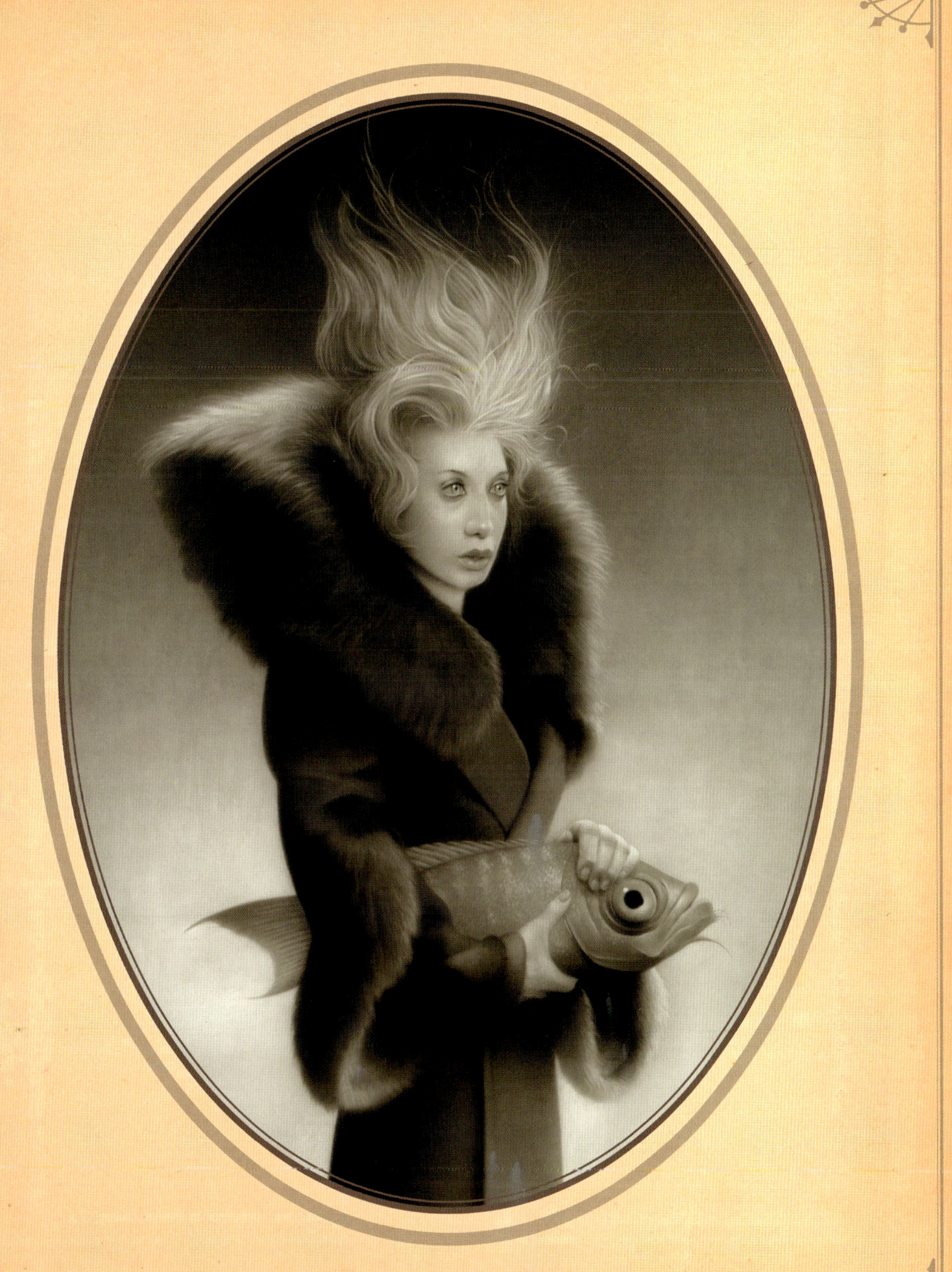

SARAH AND EMMETT

JIM WAS A PRIZEWINNING RAT CATCHER AND GIFTED PHRENOLOGIST. AFTER spending years examining the bumps on his own head, he came to the conclusion that rat catching was not the job he was best suited for.

In 1850, he was dispatched to Brixton Prison to use his phrenology skills to examine the heads of the inmates in the hope that he might get some insight into the "criminal mind." His studies were inconclusive, but while he was there, he managed to rid the prison of its rats.

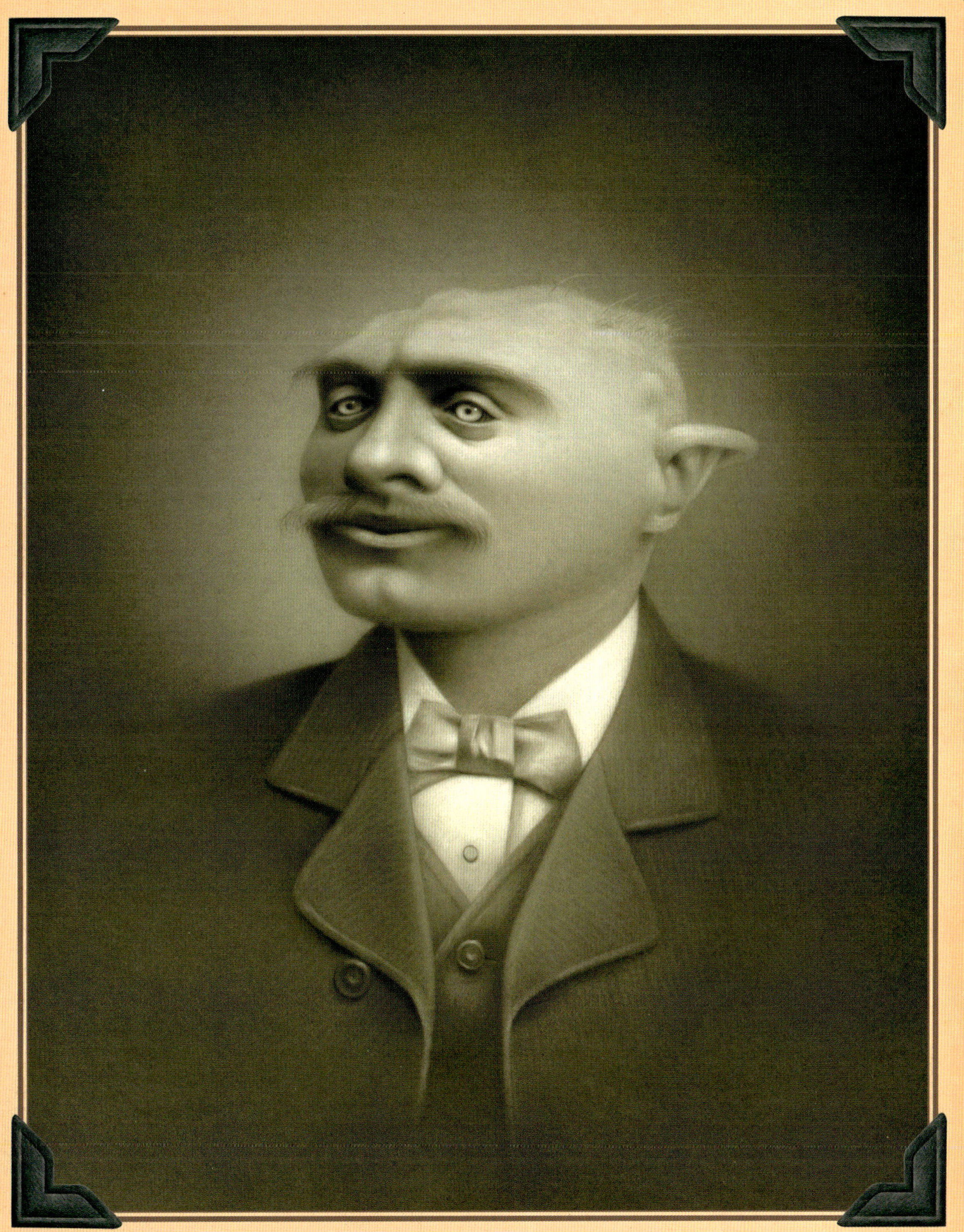

Jim "Lumpy" Phelps

EDWARD WAS AN ENGINE DRIVER WHO HAD AN OBSESSION WITH MACHINES, particularly ones that made loud, rhythmic noises. His warehouse apartment was full of old steam-driven machines. He would tinker with them when he wasn't driving his train route.

Through most of his adult life, he operated on very little sleep. But when he did allow himself to catch a few winks, his loud, unconscious tremors would vibrate his body to such a degree that, oftentimes, he would wake up several feet away from where he had lain down to rest. He once woke up down the street from his apartment. After he accidentally ran over the neighbor's cat during a particularly fitful slumber, he decided that he had to chain himself to some support beams before going to sleep at night.

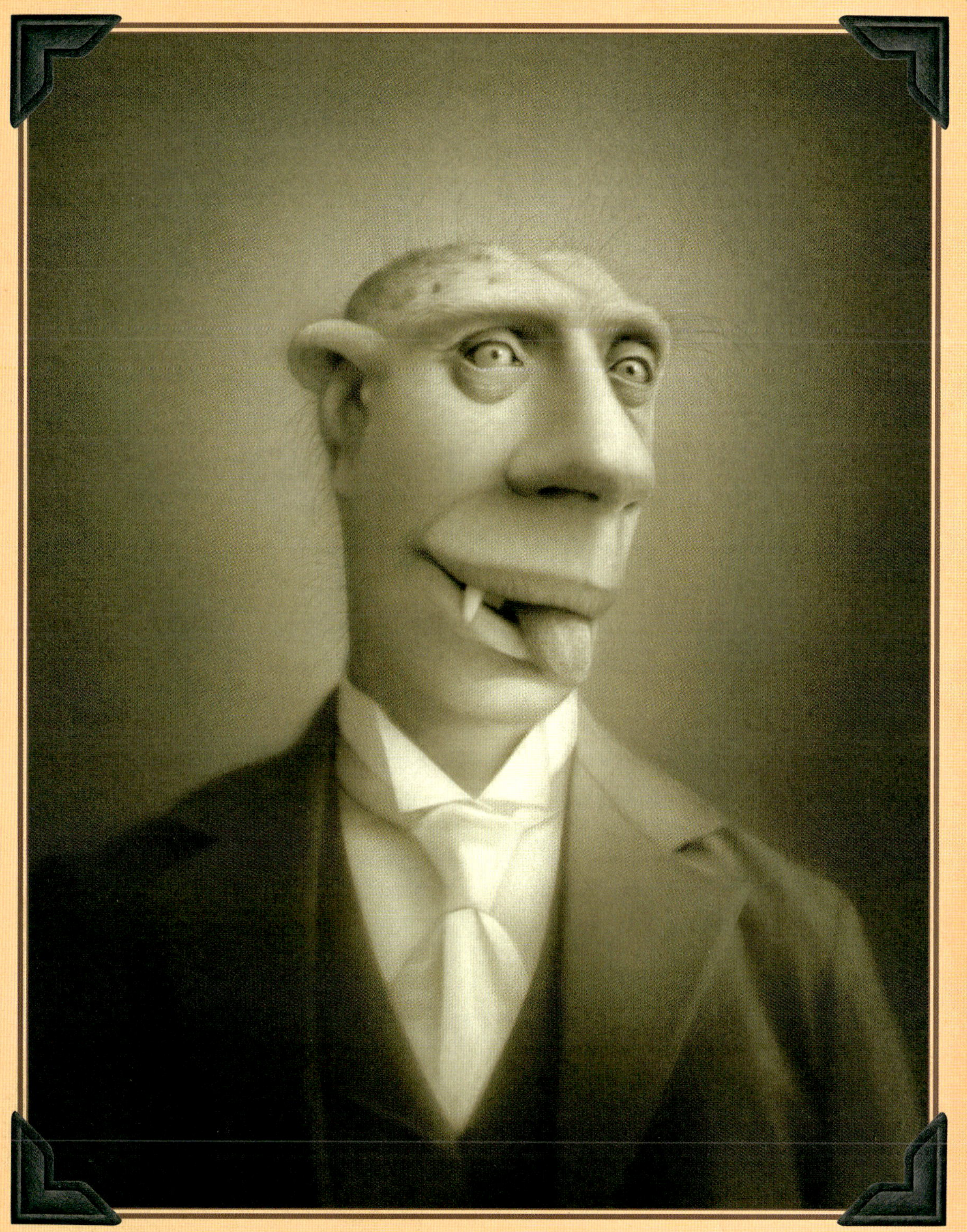

Edward "Twitchy" Jones

FRANK WOULD OFTEN SPEND HOURS LURKING NEAR CROWDED TRAIN STATIONS watching people. When his glassy-eyed stare would come across someone that he really wanted to "make friends" with, he would follow that person. He wasn't very quiet about it. He would walk just a few feet behind them . . . usually shouting at the top of his lungs . . . advice about finances, fashion, and the latest technological advances that would be helpful in this complicated modern world. He once followed a man for seven years.

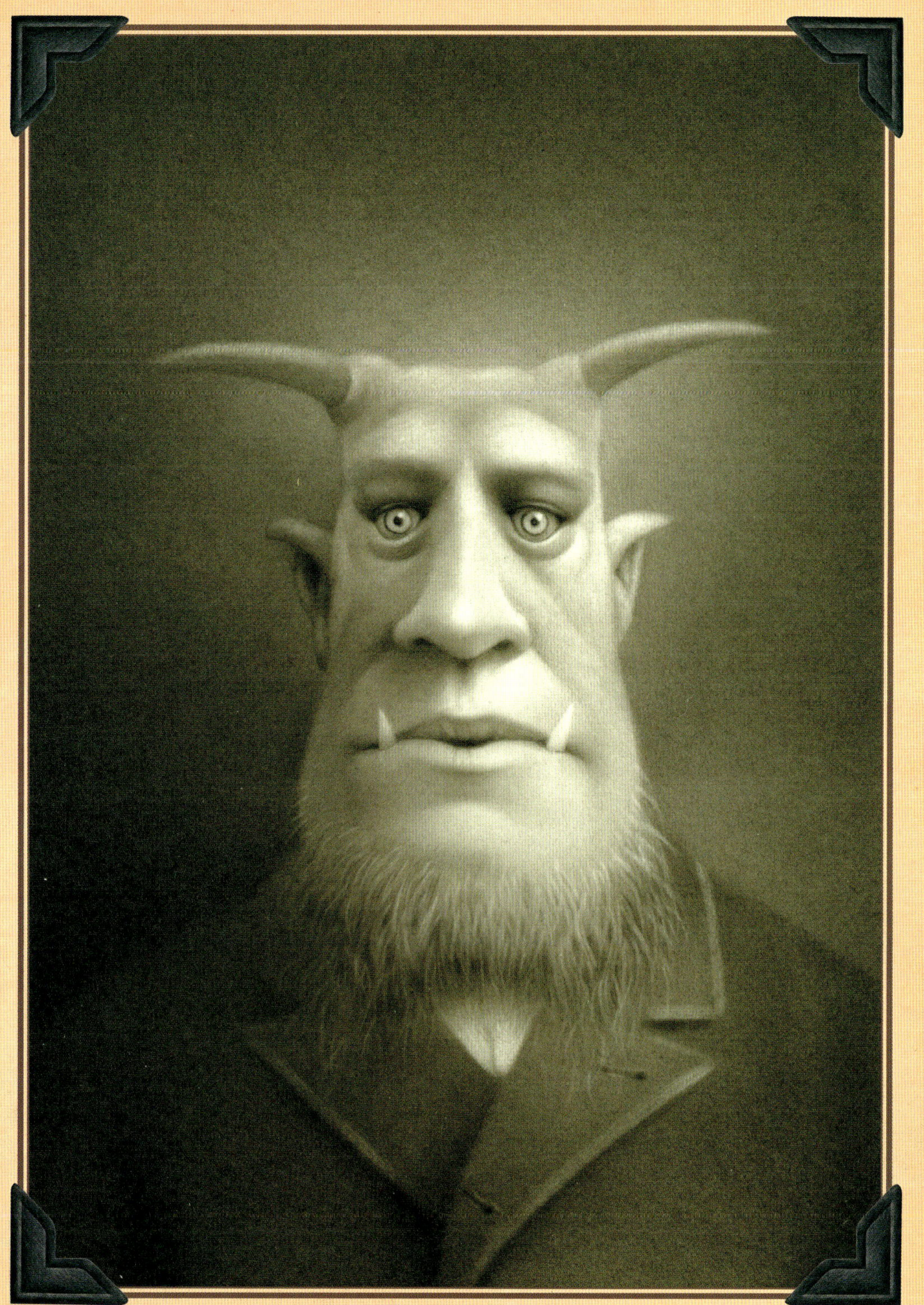

FRANK CIRCA 1897

KARL WAS DISCOVERED WORKING AS A SERVANT FOR A MOSTLY BLIND ARISTOCRAT who had recently returned from India. When members of the Zoological Society came by her home asking for donations, they noticed Karl's peculiar ape-like appearance. The aristocrat had no idea what they were talking about. She thought Karl's tanned, weathered appearance was a result of his work as a day laborer. She had thought his prodigious facial hair was unusual, but since he seemed to follow direction so easily, she had never questioned whether or not he was a man.

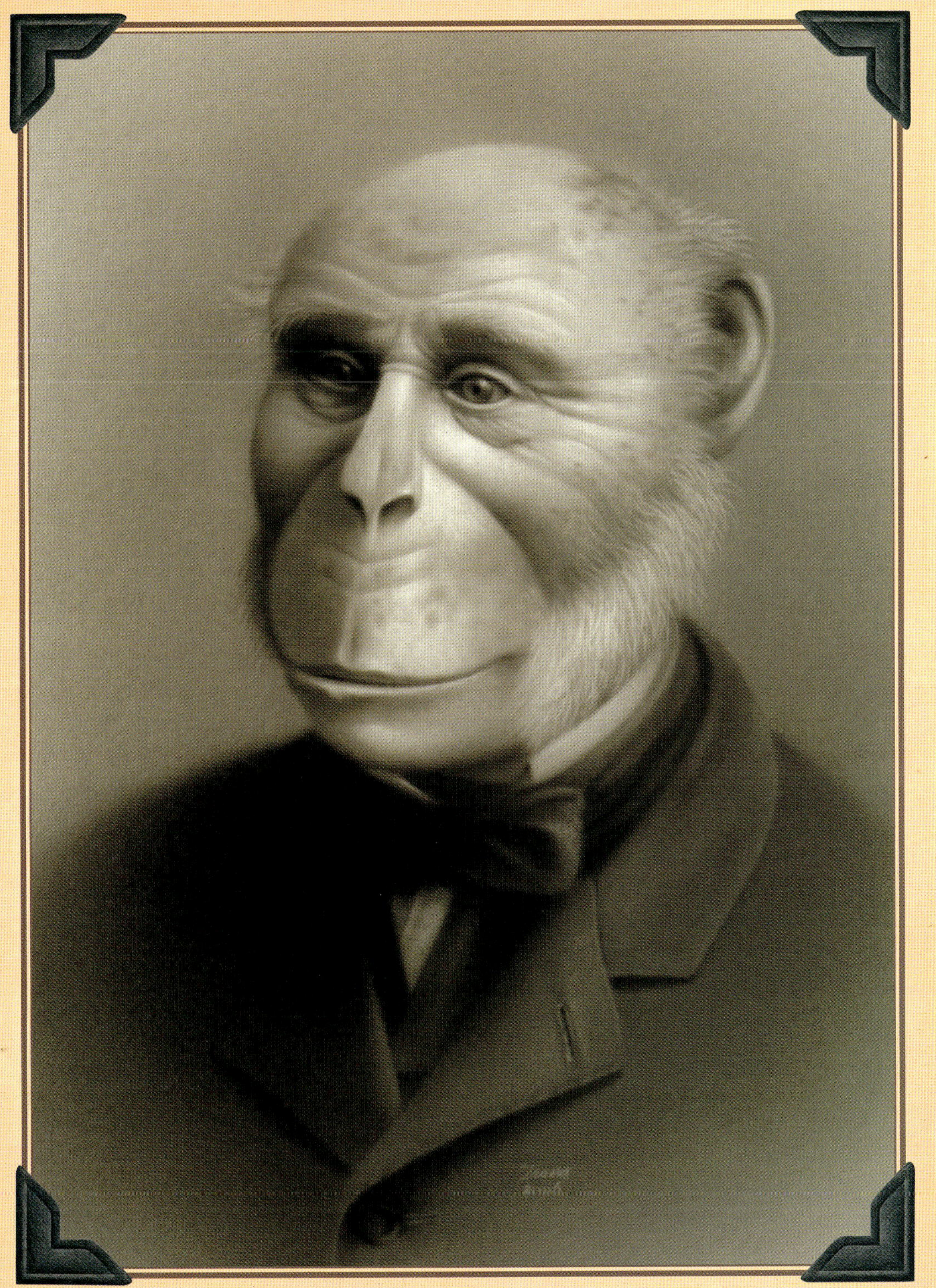

- ❧ KARL THE HUMANZEE ☙

After an explosion in a coal mine, Myron Hastings suffered a massive head injury that left a large hole in the top of his head and caused him to lose most of his personality. The monks who nursed him back to health placed a candle in the top of his head. He spent the rest of his life as a colorful tour guide for the region, entertaining tourists with candlelit tours of the ancient buildings.

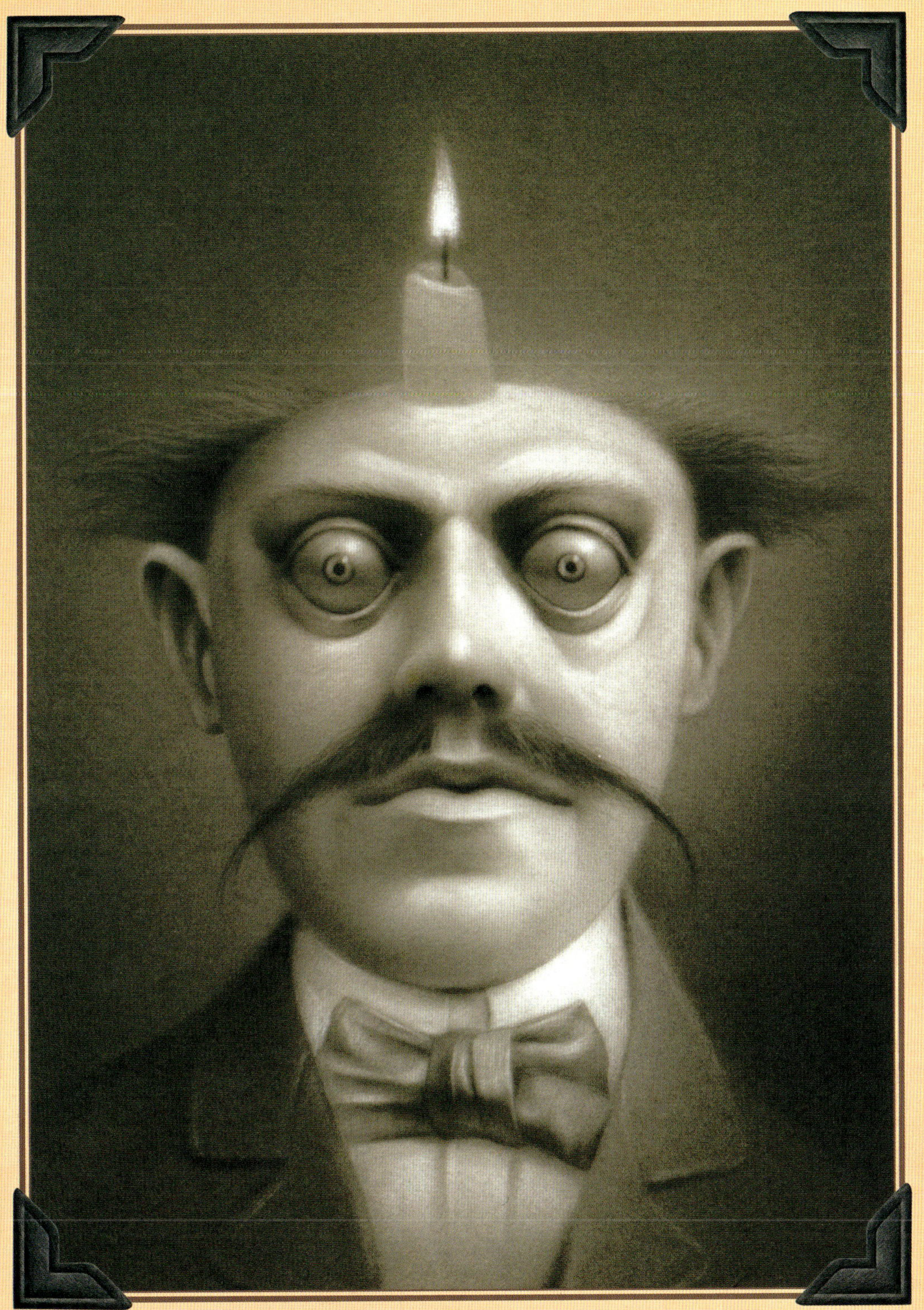

CANDLETOP HASTINGS

THE FIRST CHOKING KRAMPUS APPEARED IN 1859.

    After a long holiday season of punishing the "misbehaved" by choking or squeezing them, the Krampus would spend their "off" season gardening and landscaping. They were often seen at hardware stores and farms buying lumber, shrubs, and building materials. However, many of them were still open to be employed as chokers or stranglers . . . their services could be acquired for a nominal fee that usually included a big lunch and a light supper.

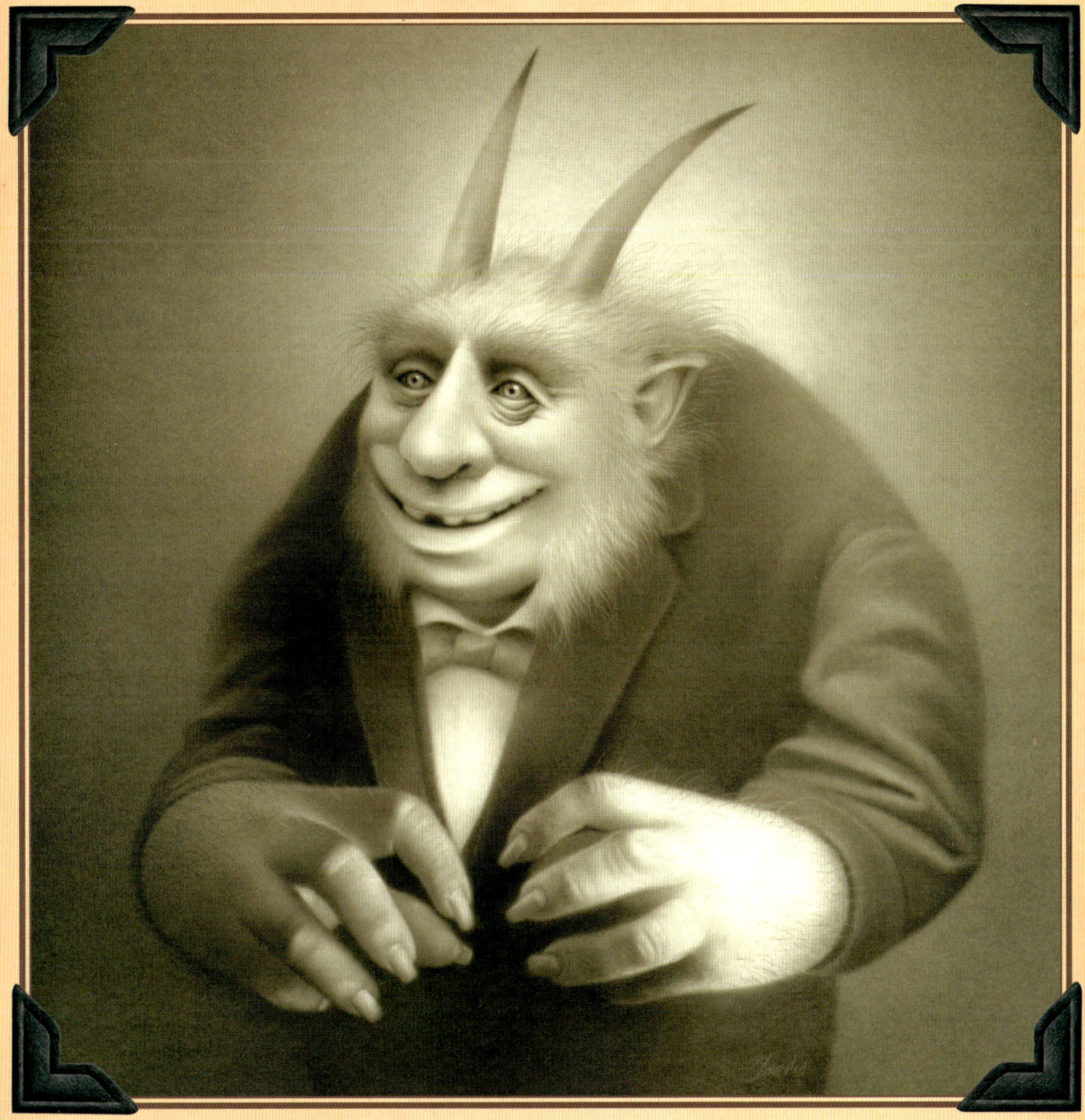

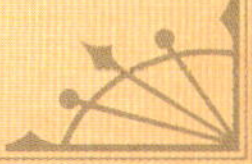

THE CHOKING KRAMPUS

THIS FASTIDIOUS KRAMPUS ALWAYS HAD A PAIR OF DISEMBODIED HANDS LEVITATING in front of himself, constantly gesturing like some vaudeville magician, even performing "slight of hand" tricks.

For the most part, he used a hypnotic gaze to put children into a trance, convincing them that they were chickens or chartered accountants working for a firm about to be audited by some large, ruthless government agency, (scary stuff).

When really bored, he simply distracted them while his disembodied hands tied their shoelaces together and poked them in the eyes.

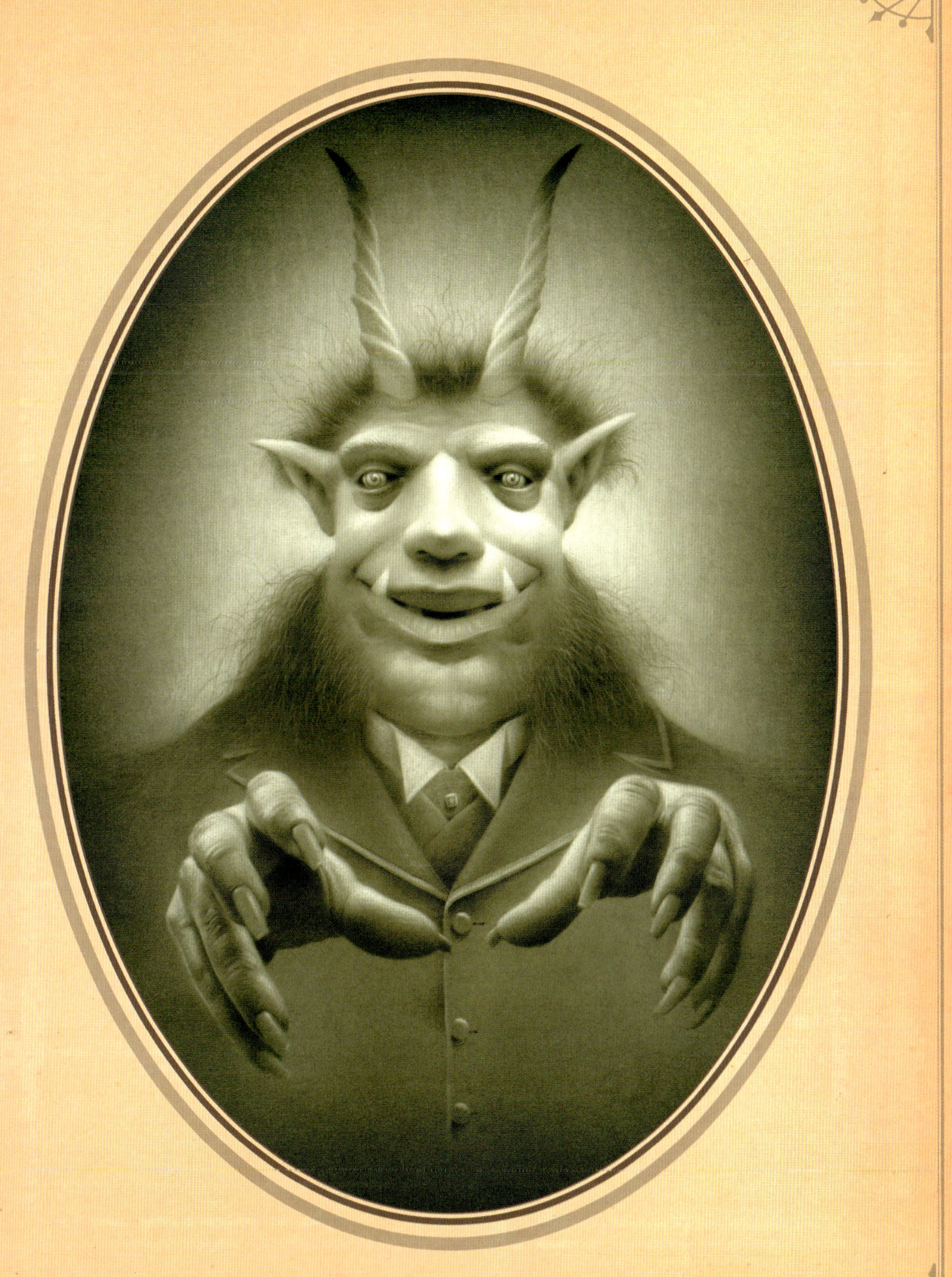

The Hypno Krampus

THE SMACKING KRAMPUS WOULD LOCATE A SUITABLE VICTIM, SNEAK UP ON HIM, and face him with an awkward silent moment. Usually, the intended victim would be paralyzed with fear.

After much deliberation the Smacking Krampus would raise his hand as if to ask a question . . . and then smack down his victim. His oversized right hand was as wide as the average frying pan.

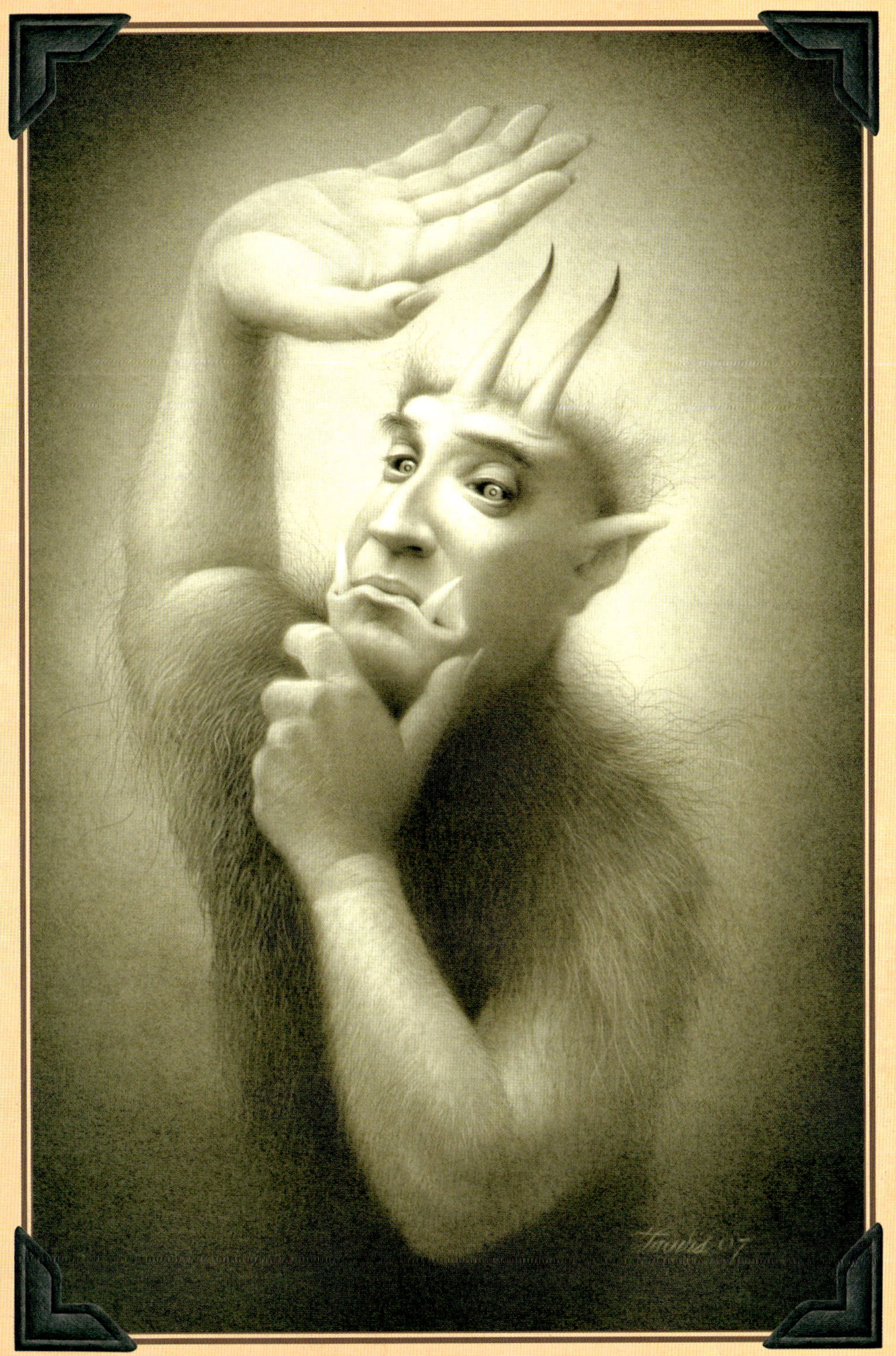

- THE SMACKING KRAMPUS -

THIS KRAMPUS PUNISHED HIS VICTIMS BY FOLLOWING THEM AROUND, USUALLY holding a wilted flower and having a sad look on his face. He would appear at important family gatherings or business meetings and embarrass his victims in front of as many people as possible. He did this by professing his undying love for them while announcing, with a loud booming voice, intimate details about their fabricated love life.

His victims included corrupt politicians, door-to-door proselytizers, overzealous tax collectors, and other people who burdened the public with their unrealistic senses of entitlement and unnecessary opinions.

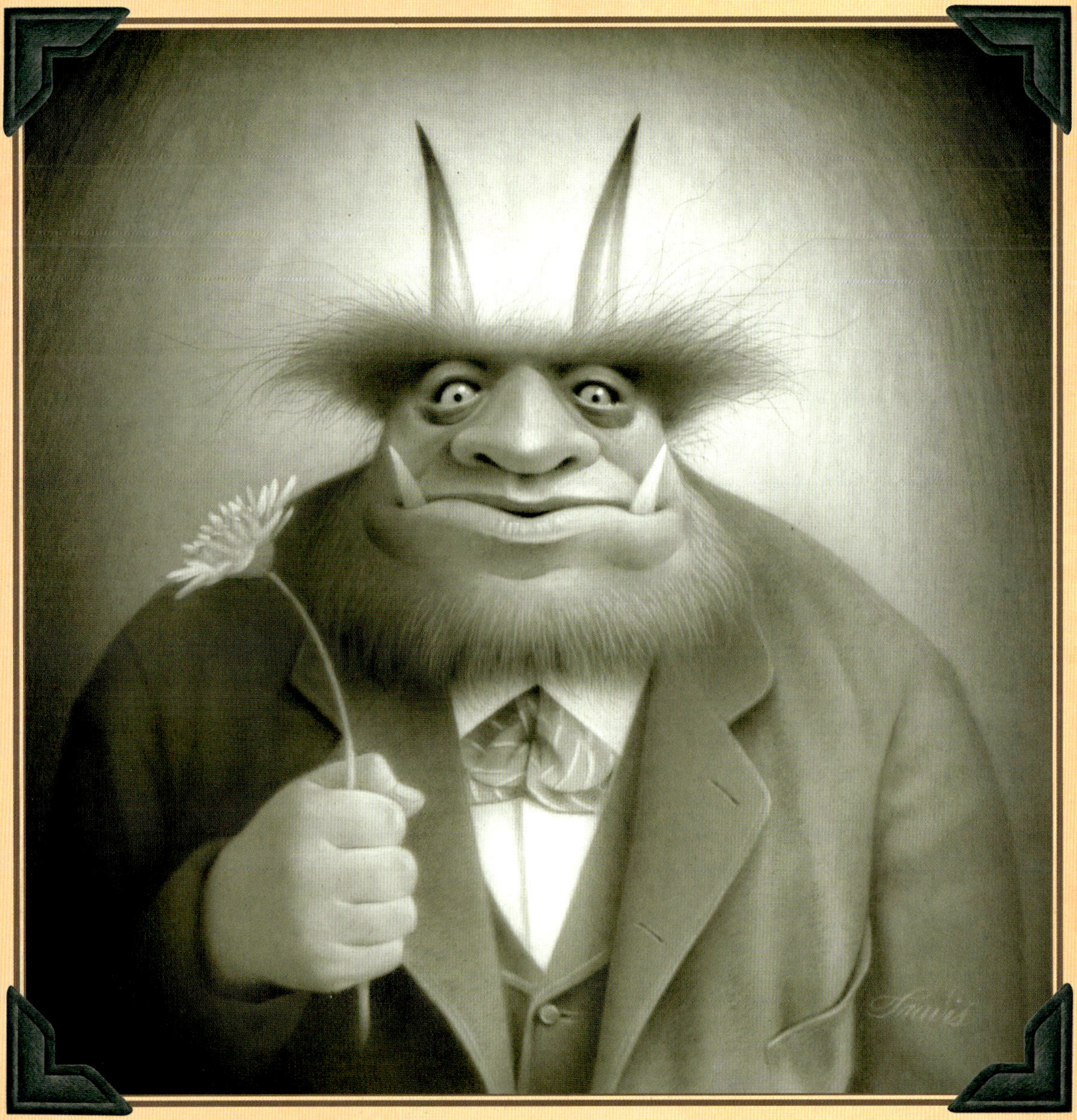

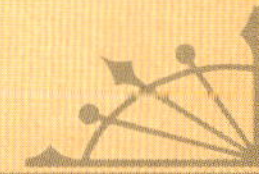

⊱ Unconditional Love Krampus ⊰

JUST BEFORE THE HOLIDAY SEASON, THERE WAS ALWAYS A LARGE GATHERING OF Krampus in Bavaria. At the conclusion of those meetings, the attendees would play "Krampus games," like stack-fighting—where the participants would climb on top of each other like totem poles, and run at full speed towards one another to try to knock each other off. The impact from such collisions would create a puff of black smoke that smelled like beer and charcoal.

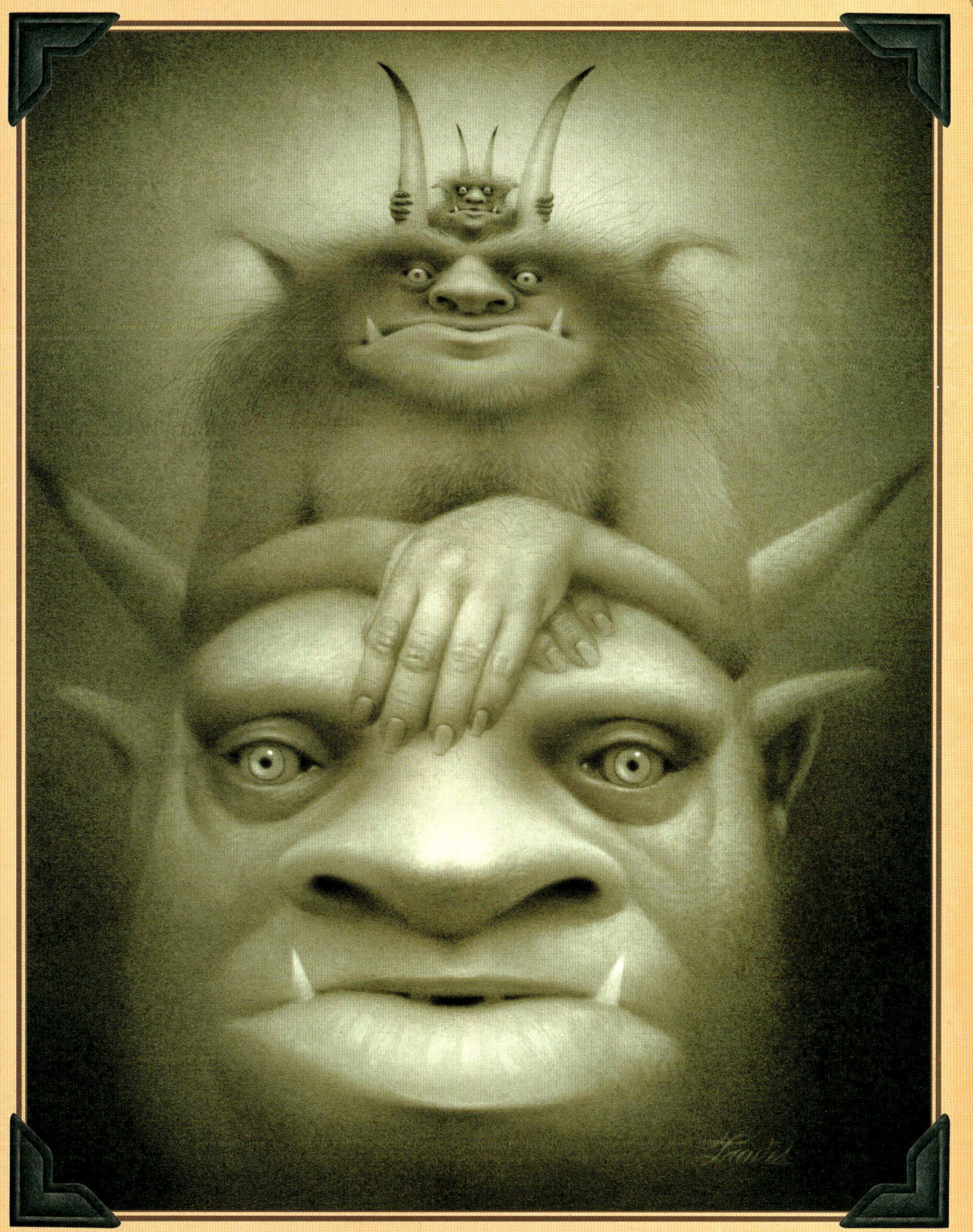

STACK OF DEMONS

SOME TIME DURING THE 18TH CENTURY, A VERY LARGE KRAMPUS IMMIGRATED to South America. He called himself the Great Gugga Mugga, because he thought the silly name would frighten people into leaving him alone. The locals made up stories about him planting "Krampus seed" in the fertile soil and harvesting full size Krampus and sending them off to eastern Europe to do his bidding.

The Great Gugga Mugga was the largest Krampus in the world. At twenty-seven feet in height, he was quite menacing.

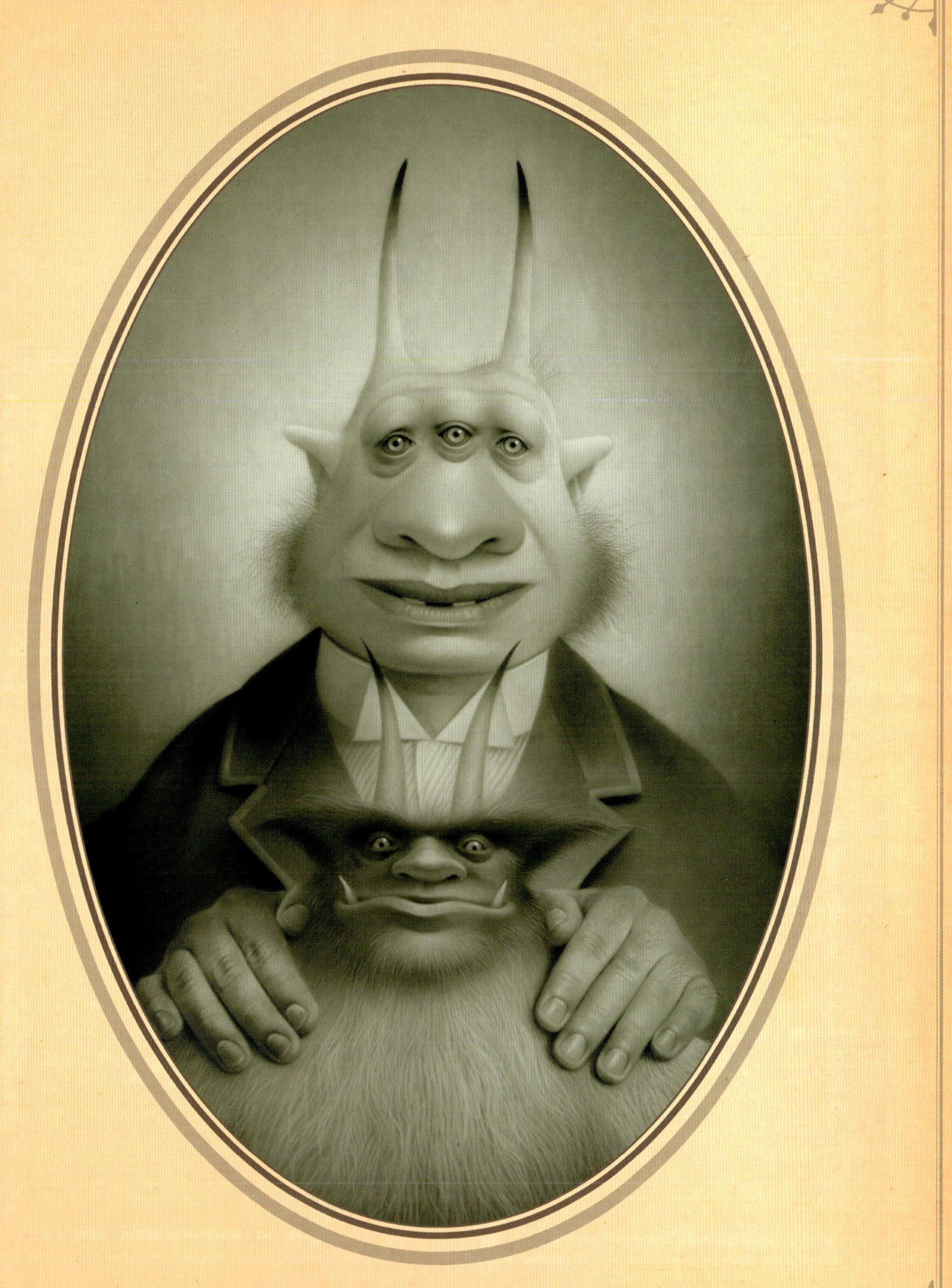

The Greater Gugga Mugga

AT ONLY THREE FEET IN HEIGHT, SAM WAS FORCED TO CARRY AROUND A FOLDING stepladder so he could reach things. Sam liked to sneak up on his victims and cover their eyes. He then whispered, in a very convincing woman's voice, words that enticed his victims to turn around. Usually they were frightened by what they encountered and fainted, at which time he cross-dressed them . . . often in evening wear. He would apply crooked wigs to their heads and mismatched high heels to their feet, (usually two left feet) and would place them in uncomfortable locations . . . usually public places like train stations or bus terminals where they would be seen by as many people as possible.

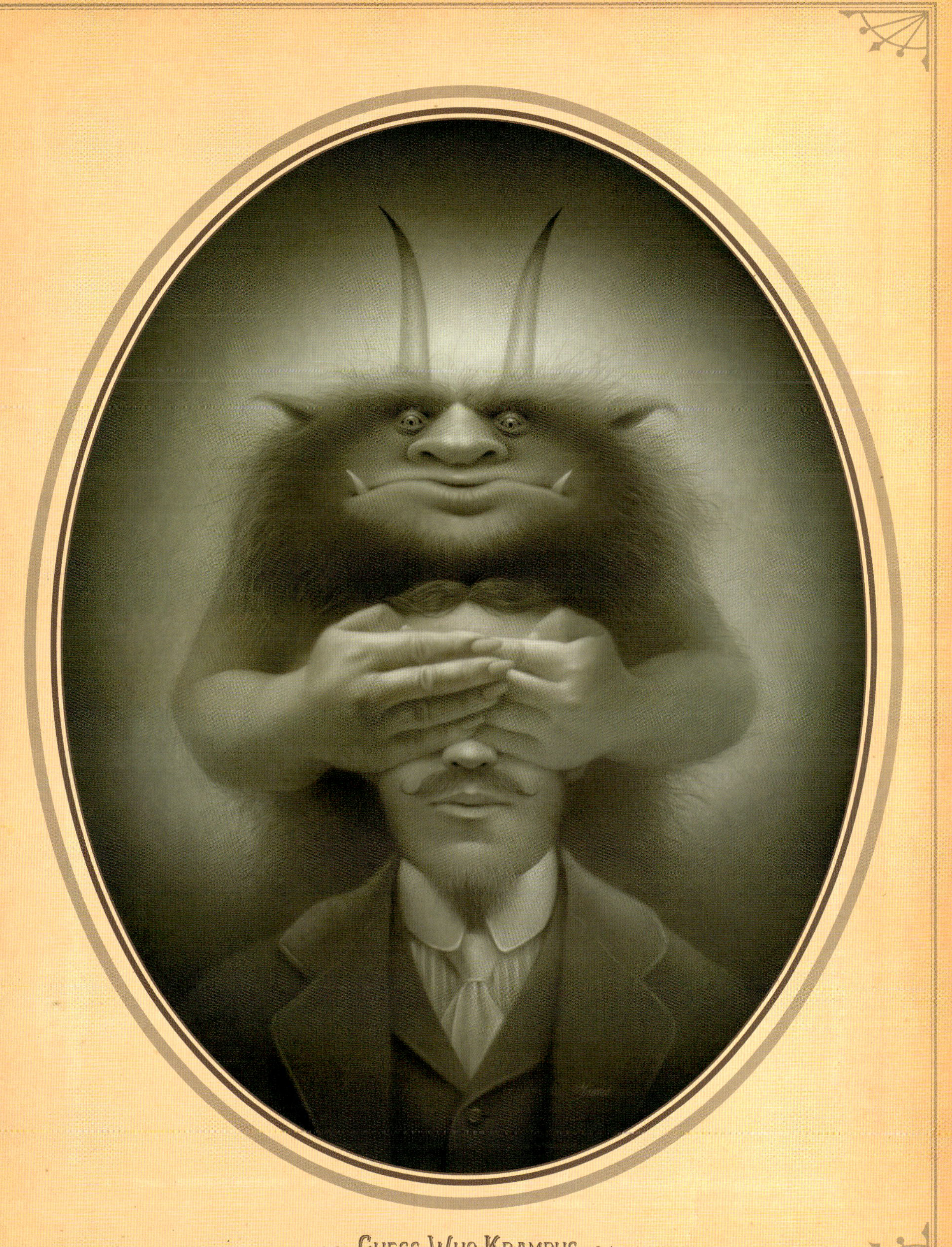

GUESS WHO KRAMPUS

Walter lost his speech when he was very young. For the rest of his life, his childhood friend, Larry, would either sit in his pocket or hide under a hat atop his head, speaking for him. Walter would mouth Larry's words, and no one ever made fun of his slightly out-of-sync, squeaky voice.

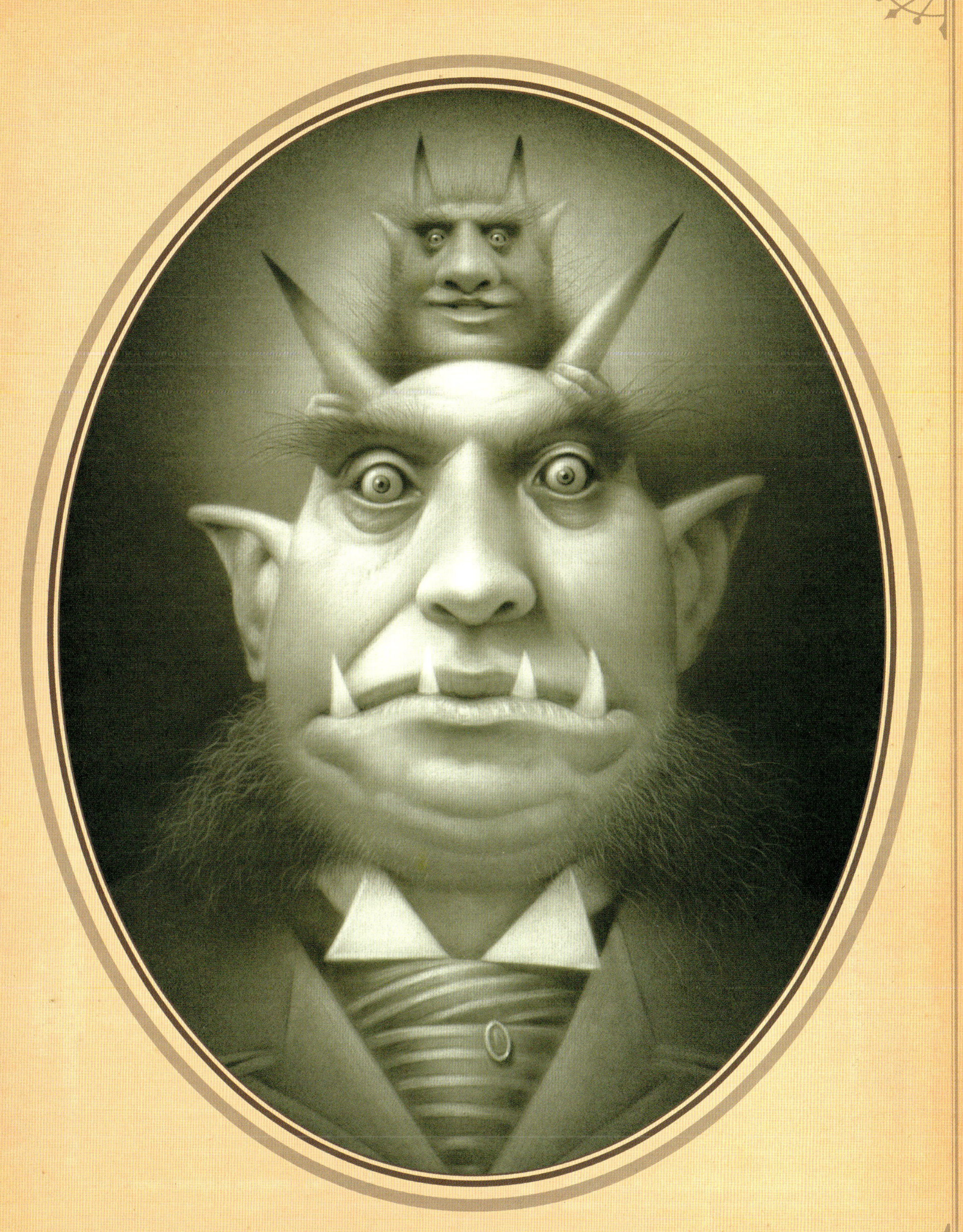

WALTER AND LARRY

BILL LIVED UNDER OTHER PEOPLE'S BEDS. WHEN HE FORGOT TO BATHE, HE SMELLED like marshmallows. He spent a great deal of his time looking in lint piles and garden beds for things to collect. He had a very large collection of lost buttons and flower seeds. He carried his most precious and shiniest buttons with him wherever he went and often left a trail of seeds in his wake. When the first spring blooms arrived, rows of mismatched flowers sprouted where he had walked the previous season.

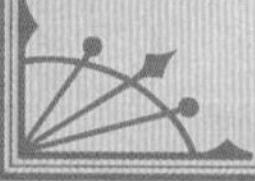

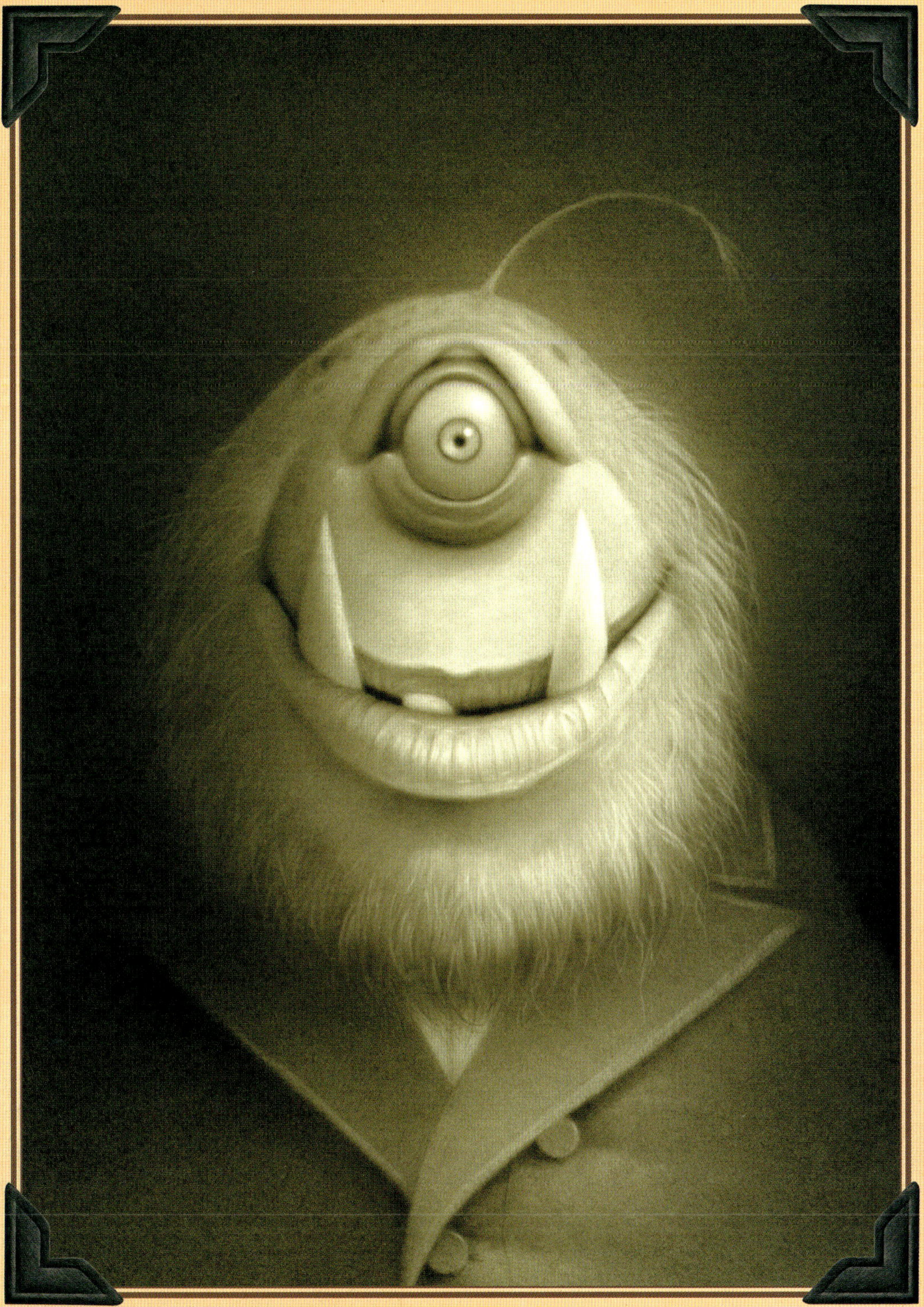

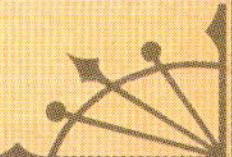

◦═ BILL ═◦

BAD VIOLIN AND CLARINET PLAYING GAVE BILL HORRIBLE HEADACHES AND MILD
hair loss. His head would swell up a few sizes and he would mumble
to himself in a low baritone. The cure for his headache was usually
mushrooms. He kept a stash of medicinal mushroom spores in his bag
. . . just in case.

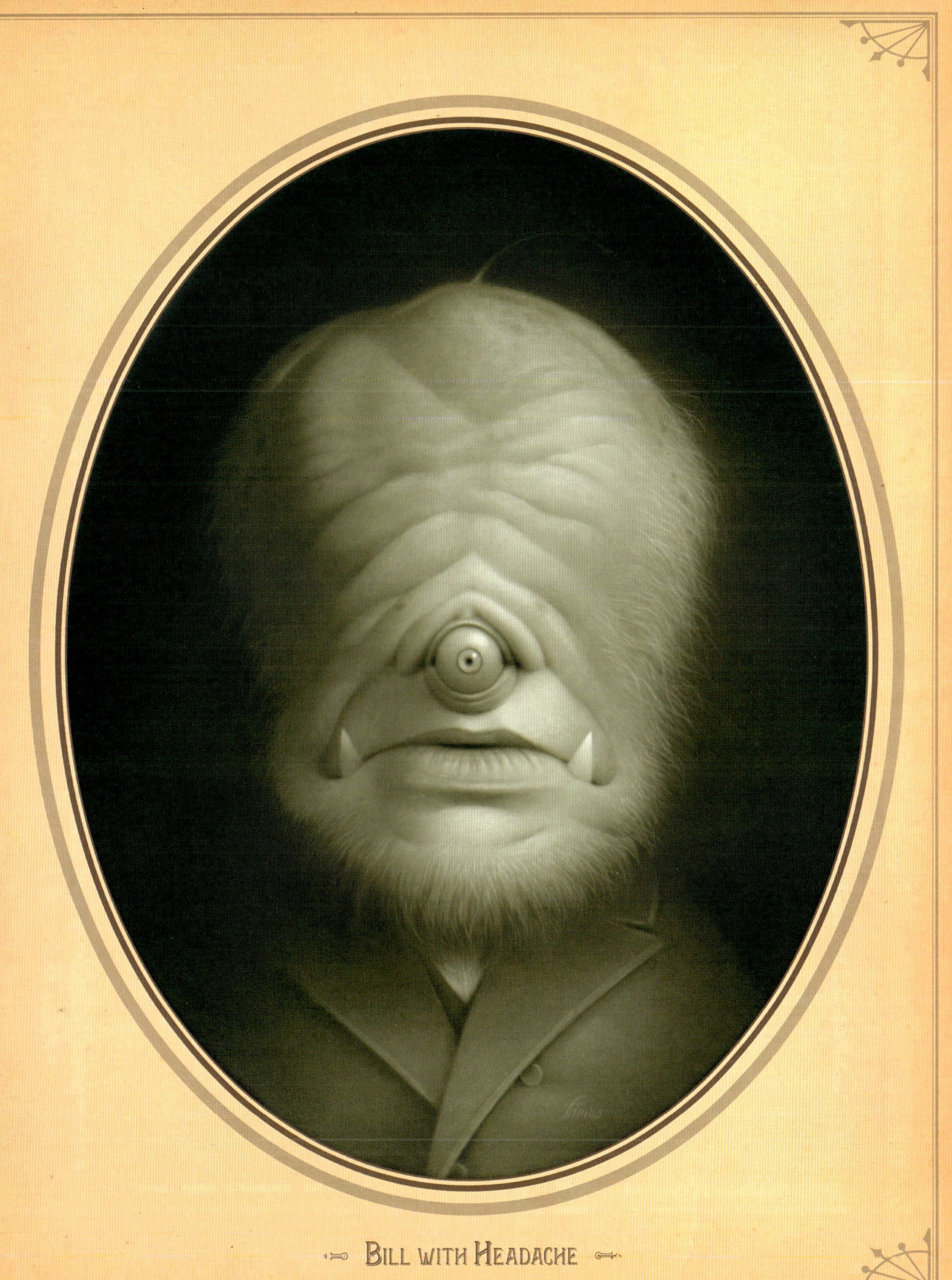

BILL WITH HEADACHE

After much consideration, Stan decided to find a wife. Her name was Judy. She lived in the places where lint collected and often created static electricity. She gave off a scent that attracted cats and voles. To throw off the scent, she rubbed herself with mushroom tonic. This made Stan very happy because he loved mushrooms.

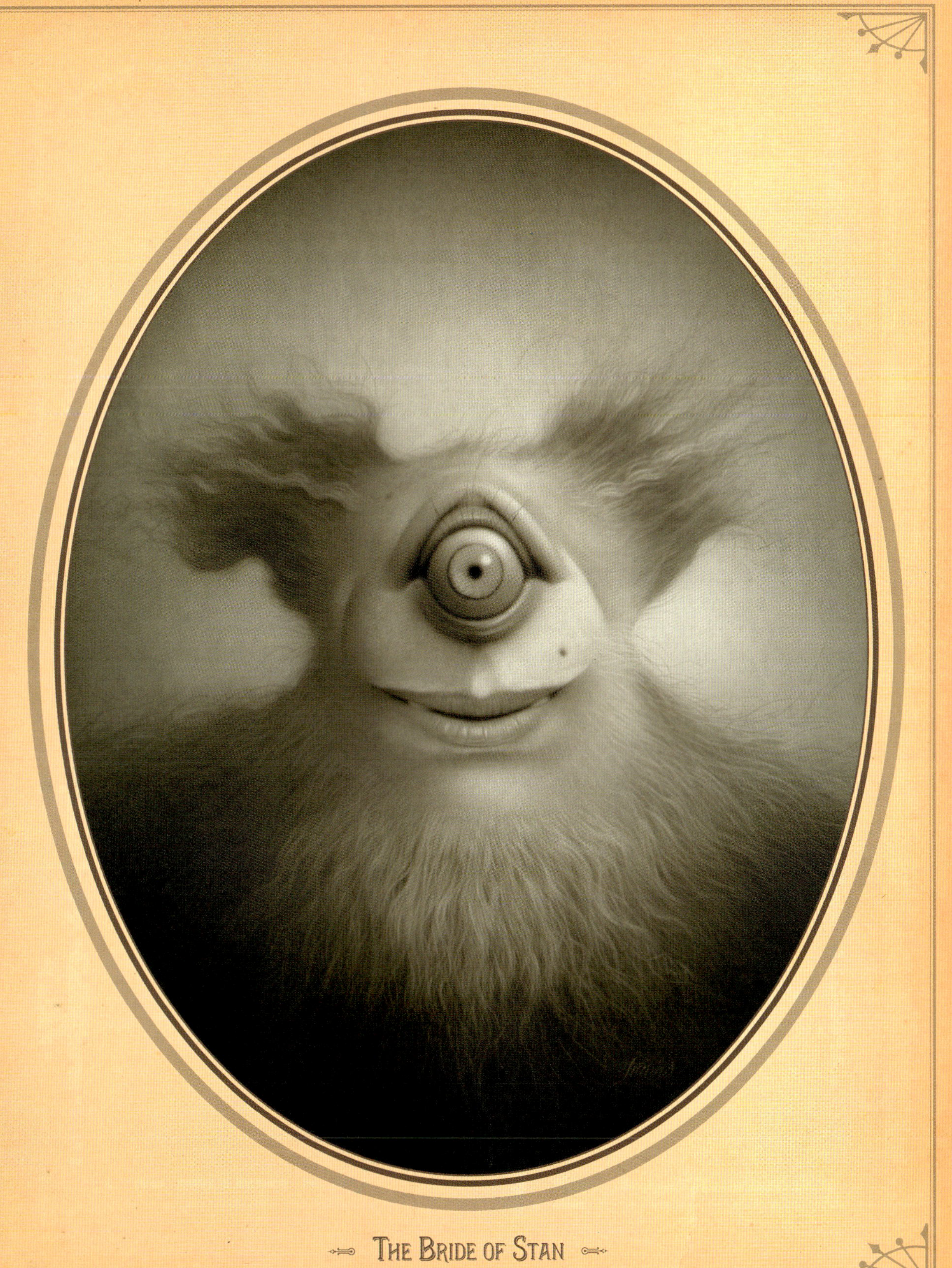

⟶ THE BRIDE OF STAN ⟵

STAN LIVED ON THE GROUND FLOOR IN A SMALL HOLE IN THE WALL JUST OUTSIDE the communal washroom. Normally Stan was covered from head to toe in hair . . . much like his wife, whom he found near the laundry room in a lint pile.

On Thursdays, at about noon, he would lose all of his hair. It would fall off with a sudden popping noise. Even though it happened every week, he was always shocked and amazed and would throw up his arms in disgust. When his arms came down, he would accidentally slap the top of his head. The sound of his hand smacking his bald head always amused him, and he would slap his head for at least twenty minutes or so before he went back to his routine.

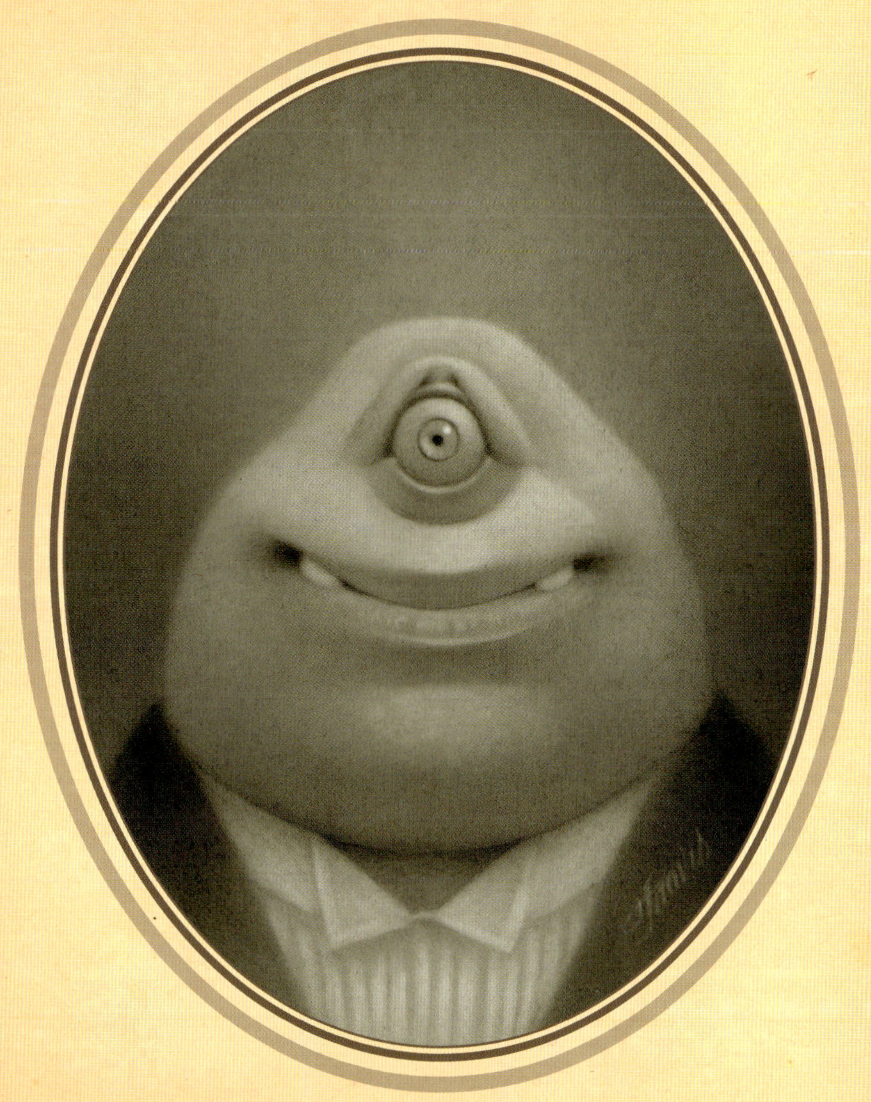

⊷ STAN BALD ⊶

DURING THE SPRING THE SEEDS THAT GOT STUCK ON BILL'S HEAD WOULD BEGIN to sprout flowers. In the evenings the blooms gave off a soft glow. His floral nightlights were mistaken for fireflies as he traveled from house to house looking for a place to sleep. Flowers would bloom on his head throughout the summer months. By the fall most of the flowers would have wilted off his head . . . except for the marigolds.

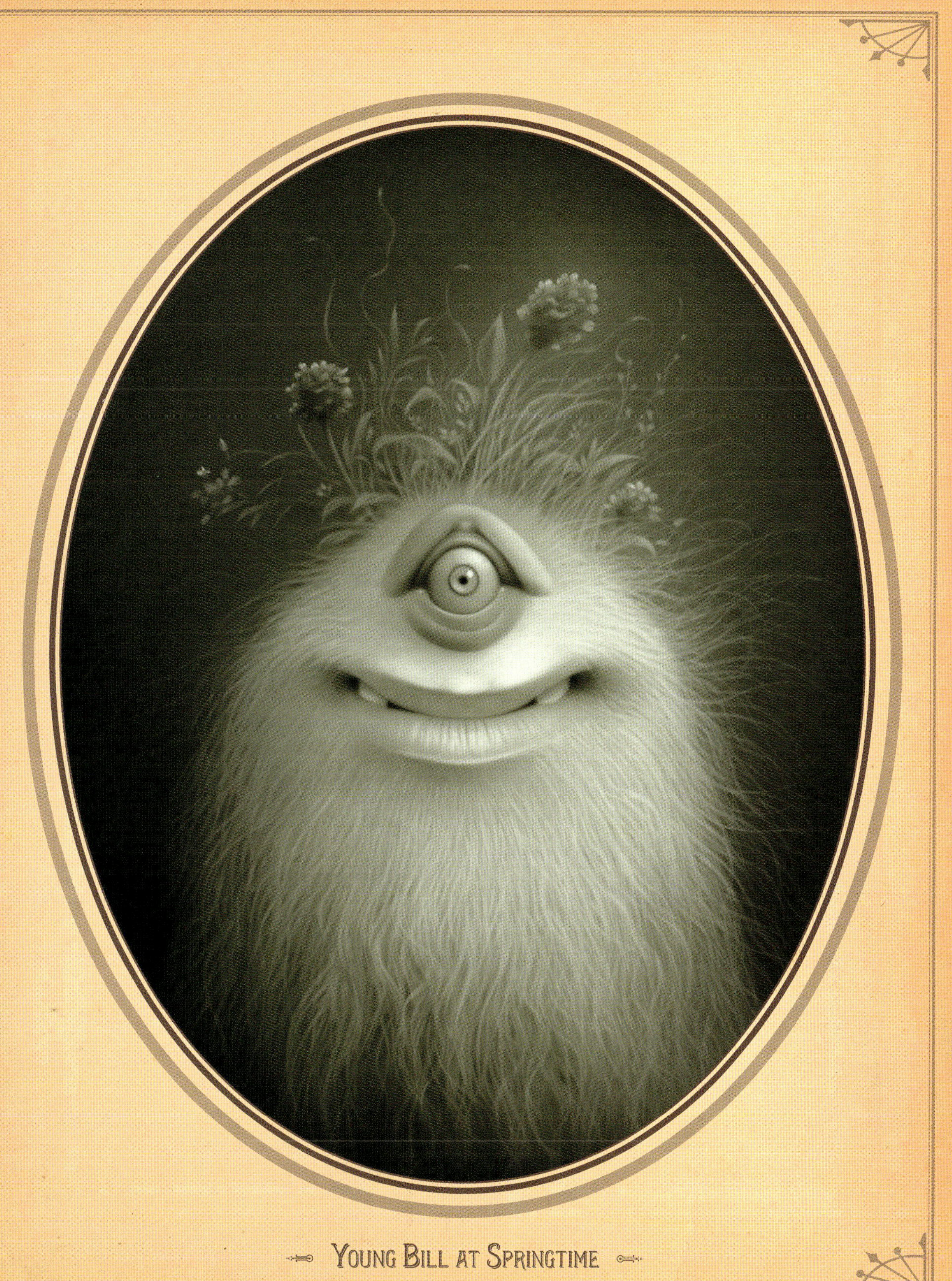

YOUNG BILL AT SPRINGTIME

BILL HAD AN UNCLE VICTOR WHO LIVED IN ASTORIA, NEW YORK. HE ALSO lived under other people's beds. When he didn't bathe, he smelled like licorice.

Despite only having three fingers on each of his hands, he was an excellent piano player. In the evenings he snuck into the local piano factory and marveled at the new pianos. One night he summoned up the courage to play one of them. He was so enraptured with the beautiful tone of the instrument that he almost didn't make it out of the factory by dawn. He was in such a hurry that he dropped his gloves. The discovery of a pair of licorice-scented, three-fingered gloves caused quite a stir the next day.

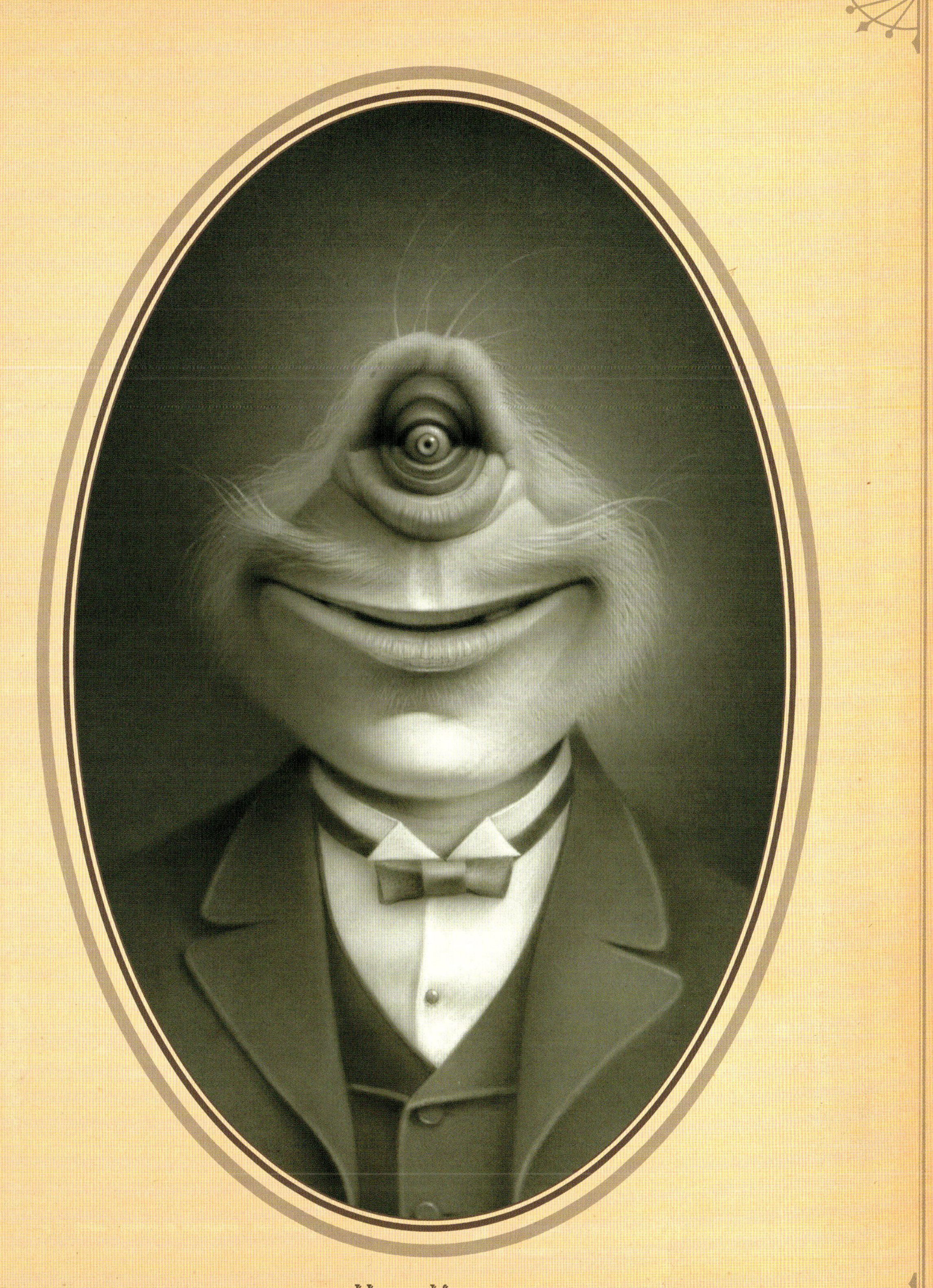

Uncle Victor

Uncle Wally spent most of his time in the forest protecting woodlands from pollution and corporate land acquisition with his magical powers. He sang awful songs all day long. His out-of-tune whistling could be heard for miles. He spoke in an uneasy voice that changed in pitch from a high squeak to a low groan. When he lost his temper, the pitch in his voice would get higher . . . in fact, the angrier he became, the squeakier his tone would be. When a lumber company came to cut down trees in his forest, he squawked unintelligibly, like an angry rooster, and he turned the team of lumberjacks into mushrooms. He devoured them for supper that evening.

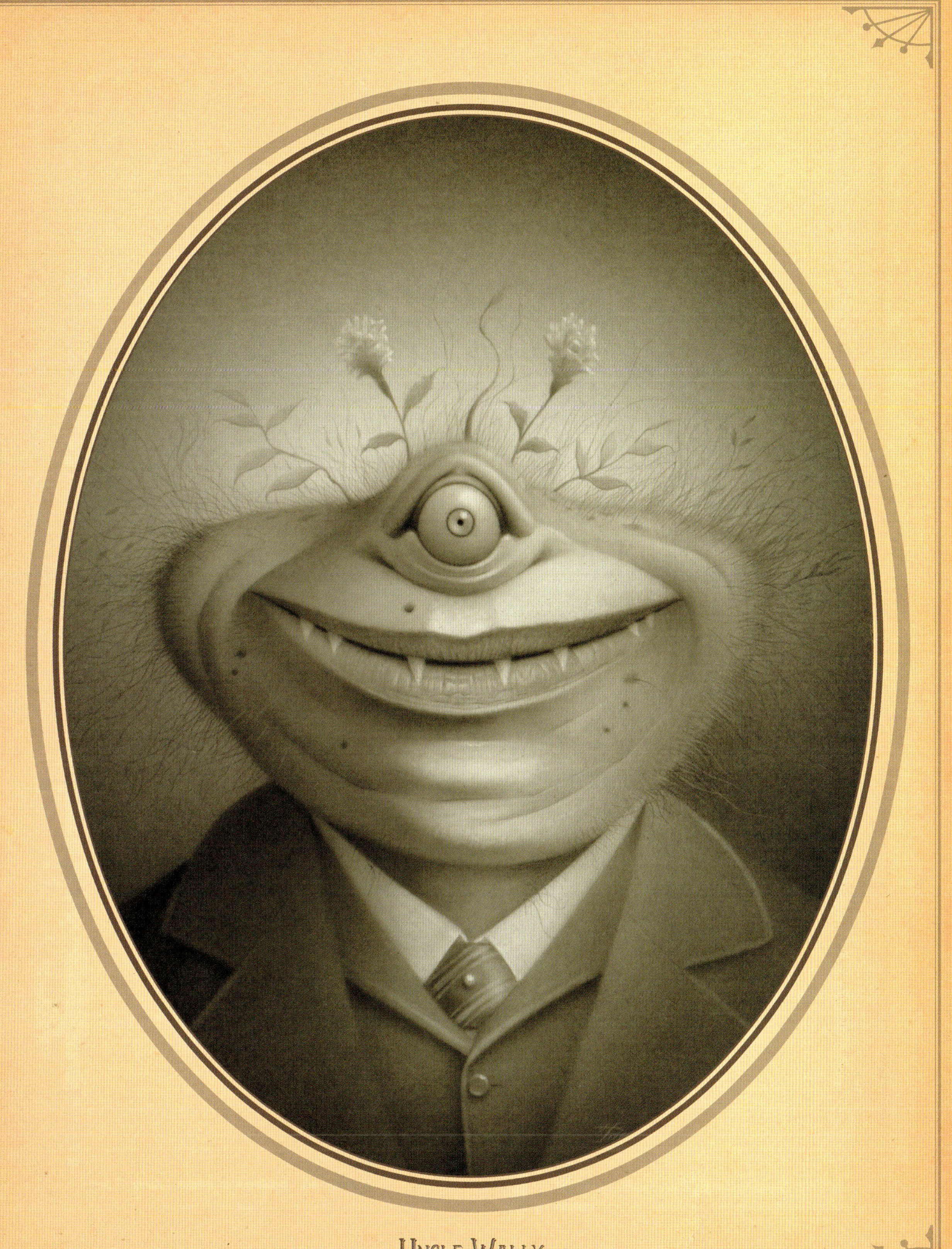

UNCLE WALLY

JENNY WINWOOD WAS MOTH-WATCHING ON A SUNDAY EVENING WHEN SHE WAS bitten by the awful Eric Smithson, of the Cobble Hill Smithsons. After a moment of shortness of breath, she discovered in her uneven reflection that she had acquired Eric's bad hair. There was not much she could do to rid herself of the bad hair . . . she tried to wash the badness out, cut it to a manageable shape, even tie it up, but to no avail. Her bad hair kept coming back.

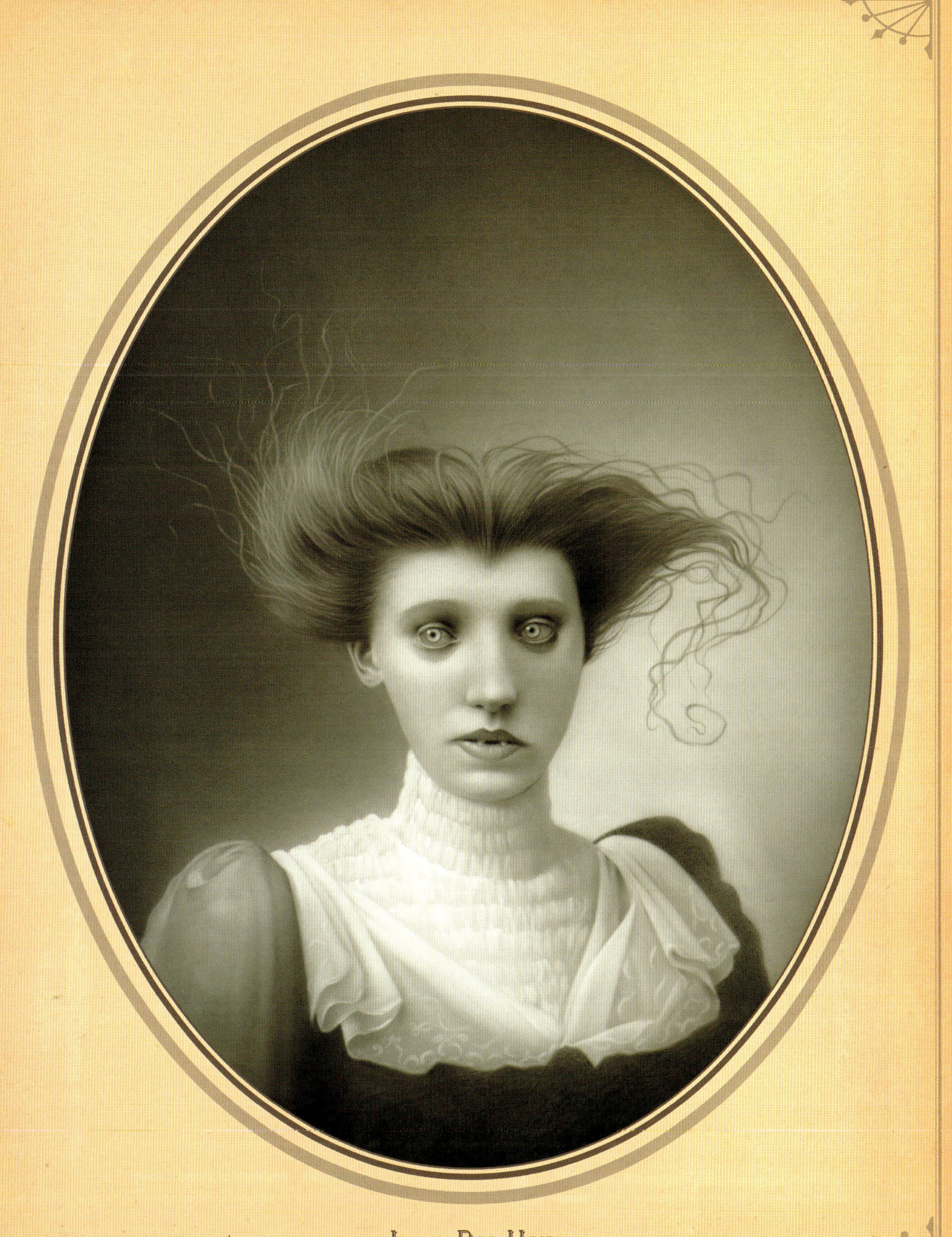

— Jenny Bad Hair —

EMILY FITZGERALD EMIGRATED FROM WALES IN 1879, AND WORKED THE SIDESHOW circuit for many years as a fortune-teller and fire-eater. Tired of traveling from town to town, she decided to move to New York and found work in Coney Island's Dreamland. She was part of the Hell Gate exhibition. When the park burned down in 1911, she went to Chicago and developed a stage act that eventually went on tour. She returned to New York and played in the Catskills in the 1930s.

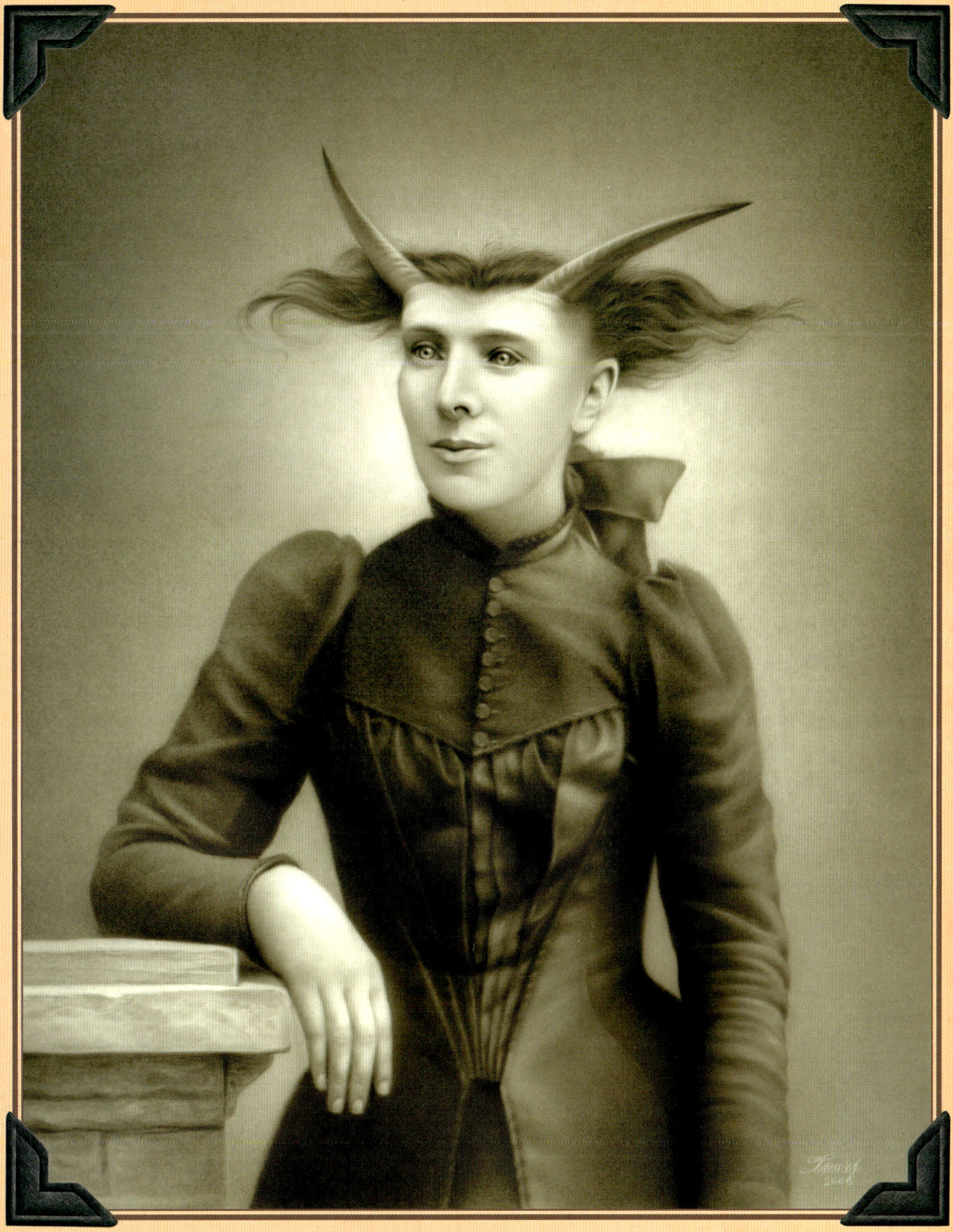

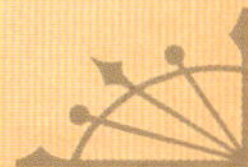

◦⇾ EMILY ⇽◦

Eunice pulled herself out of the ground during the great potato famine sometime around 1847. After an unsuccessful search in the local towns, she decided to head for North America to find a man.

It is said that she was quite a conversationalist and a fantastic dancer. Some stories suggest that she found a man in New Paltz, New York. Other accounts have her settling in Stanfordville, New York, with a sheep farmer.

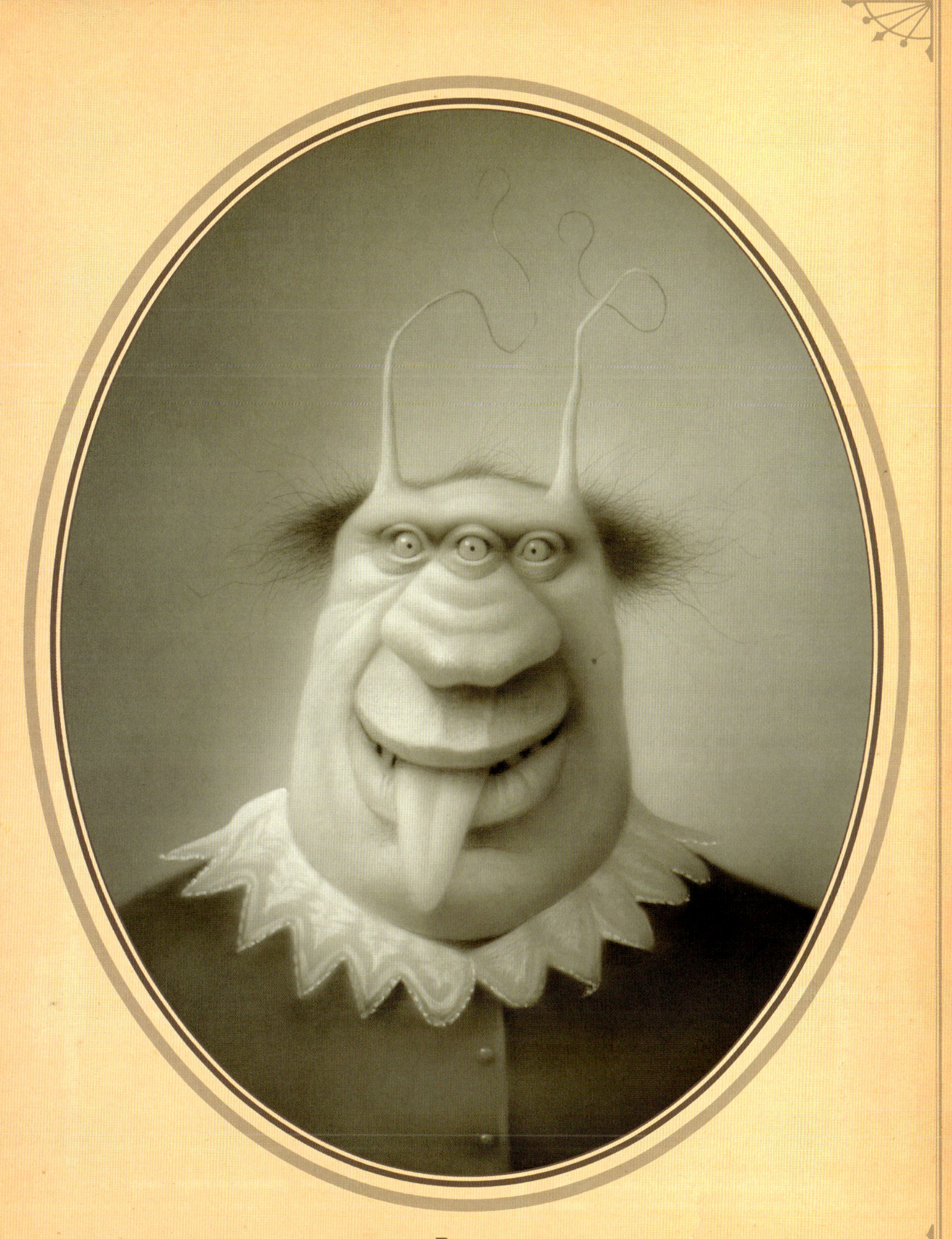

Eunice

NOT MUCH WAS KNOWN ABOUT THE AMPHIBIAN KNOWN AS GLEN. SOME SAY HE
came out of the Hudson River to buy real estate in Brooklyn. Others say
he came from the traveling carnival circuit and settled in New York when
Dreamland opened in Coney Island.

We do know that he lived in an apartment on Mulberry Street in
Lower Manhattan and that he mysteriously disappeared in 1925. After a
heavy rainstorm in 1939, he reappeared at his apartment. The new tenants
were surprised when he came out of the wall.

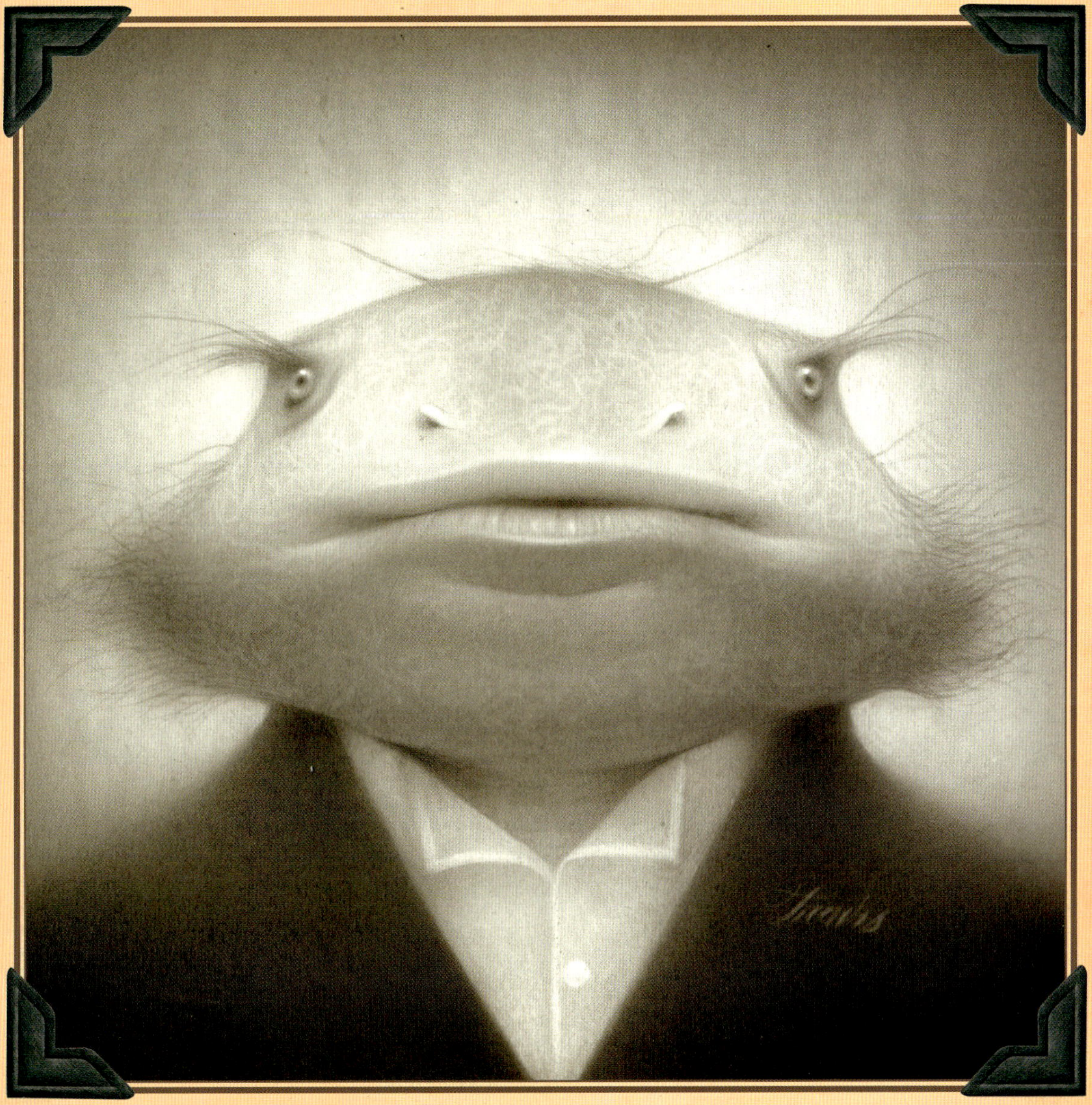

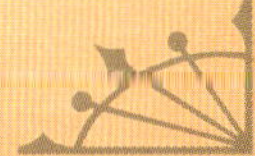

— GLEN —

Mr. Grimace always wanted his picture taken, but the flash powder always made his hair stand up. He was mostly sad because he lost his wife to a hedge-cutting accident. The sound of hedge clippers always made him cry.

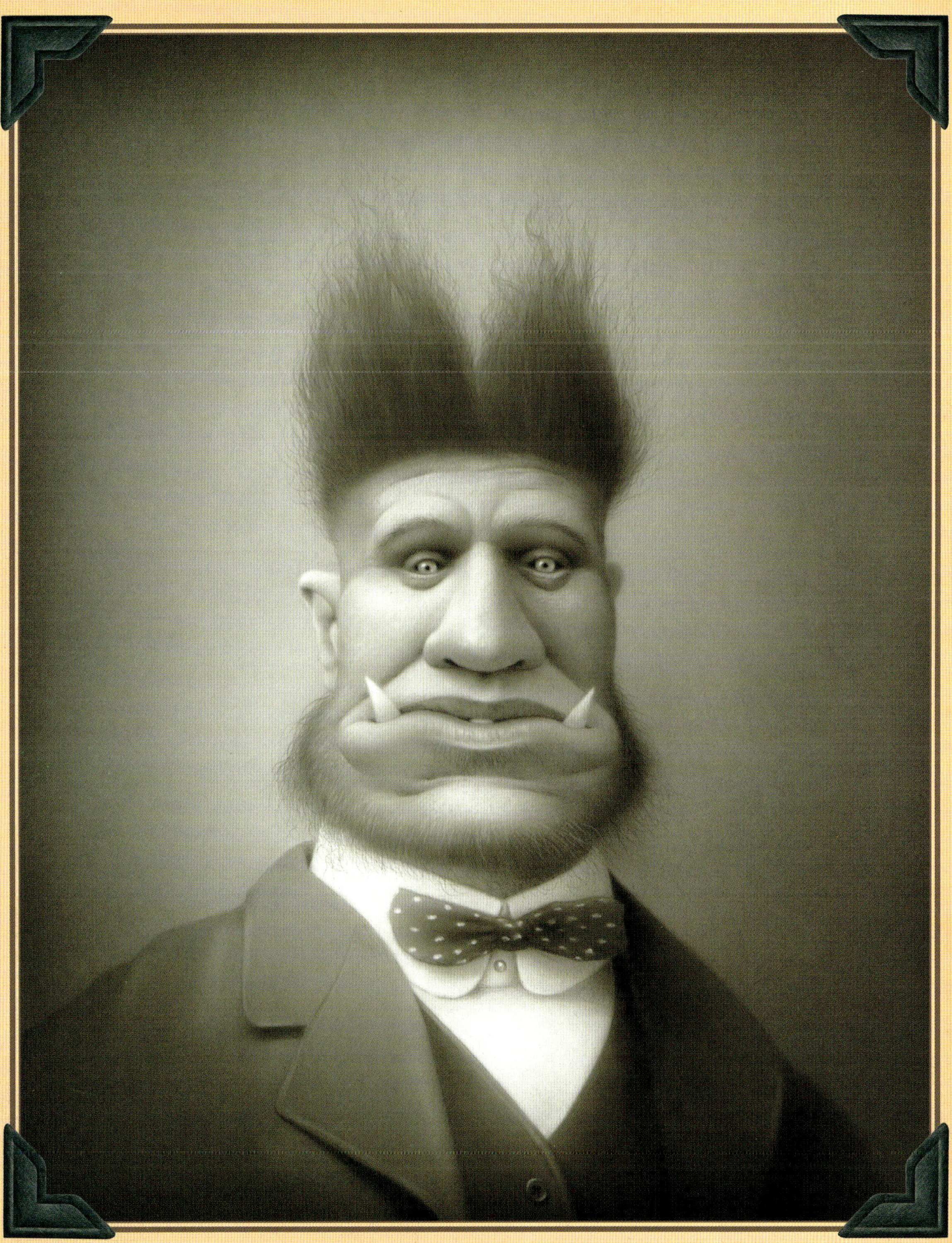

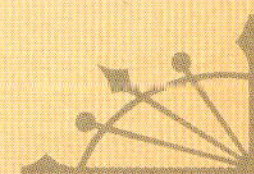

— ⊷ Sad Mr. Grimace ⊶ —

MARVIN LIVED IN THE CELLAR OF HIS PARENTS' HOUSE . . . LIKE MOST SIX-EYED people in the 19th century. He was very friendly and always had kind words for everyone he met, except for tax collectors, who often put him in an uncontrollable rage. Every year the local assessor had to be replaced; either he went missing or was found bound and gagged in the trunk of an old tree.

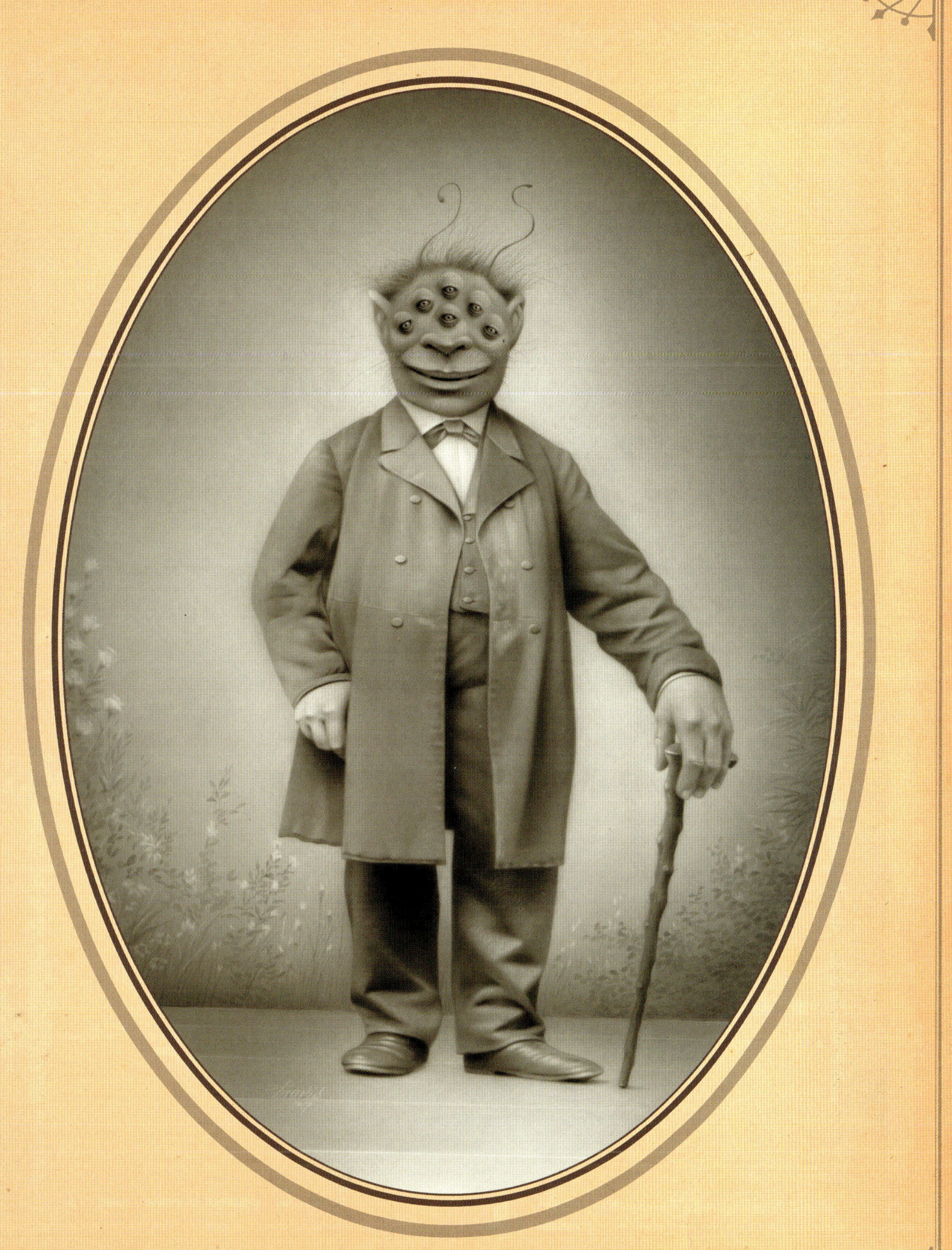

MARVIN

MAXO WAS A FORTUNE-TELLER. THROUGH PALM READING AND MIND CONTROL techniques, he could tell someone's future or convince them to change it. If he was paid one penny he would tell a fortune; if paid two pennies, he would tell that same fortune twice.

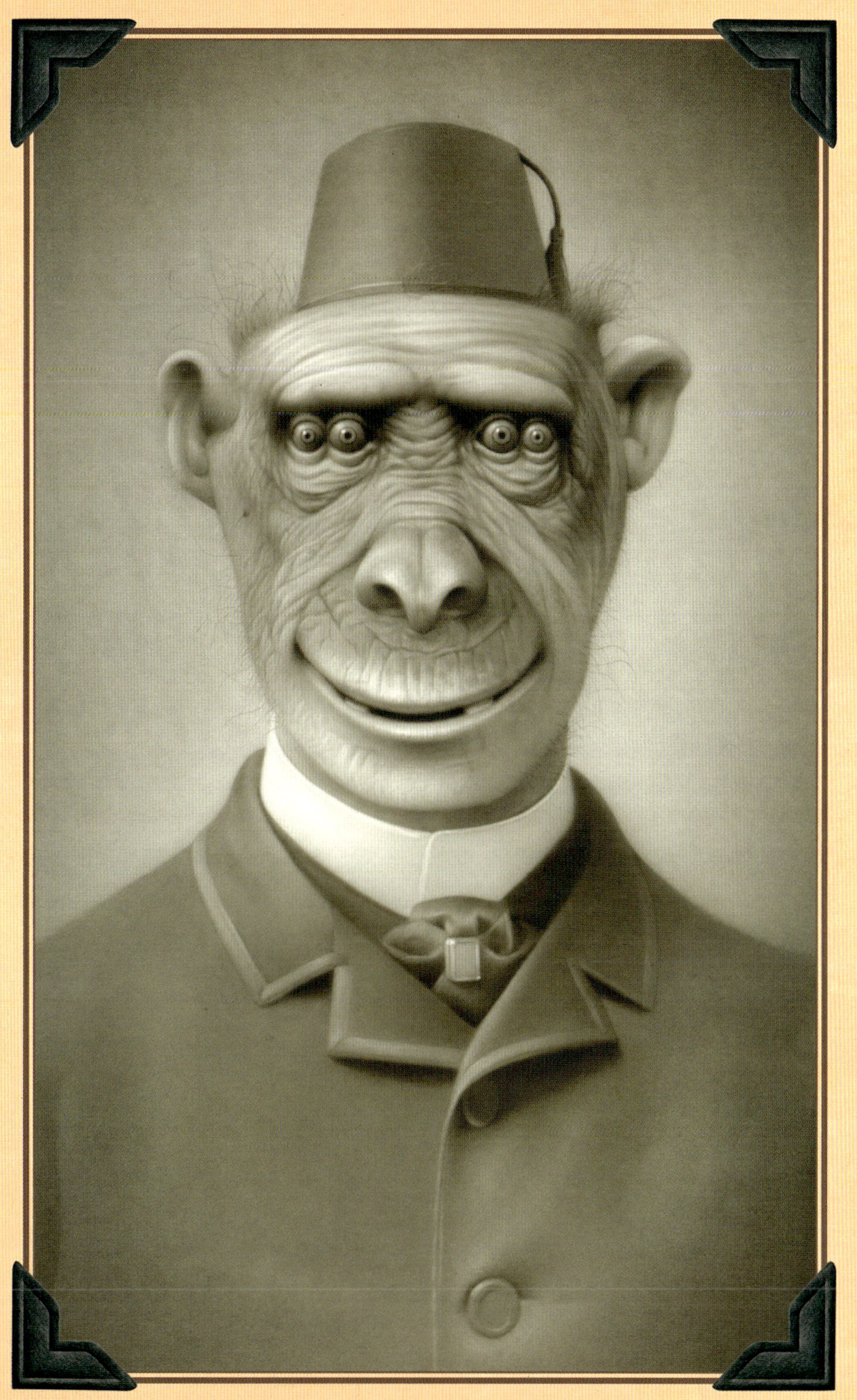

Maxo The Ultra Chimp

MARTIN WAS THE FIRST GIBBON TO BE NAMED HEADMASTER AT BELHAVEN HILL IN Dunbar. His specialty was anthropology, but he was also very knowledgeable about combustion engines. When the first automobiles became available to the public, he was the first instructor of auto mechanics in Dunbar. Sadly, he was run over by one of his own students and was forced to retire just before the Second World War.

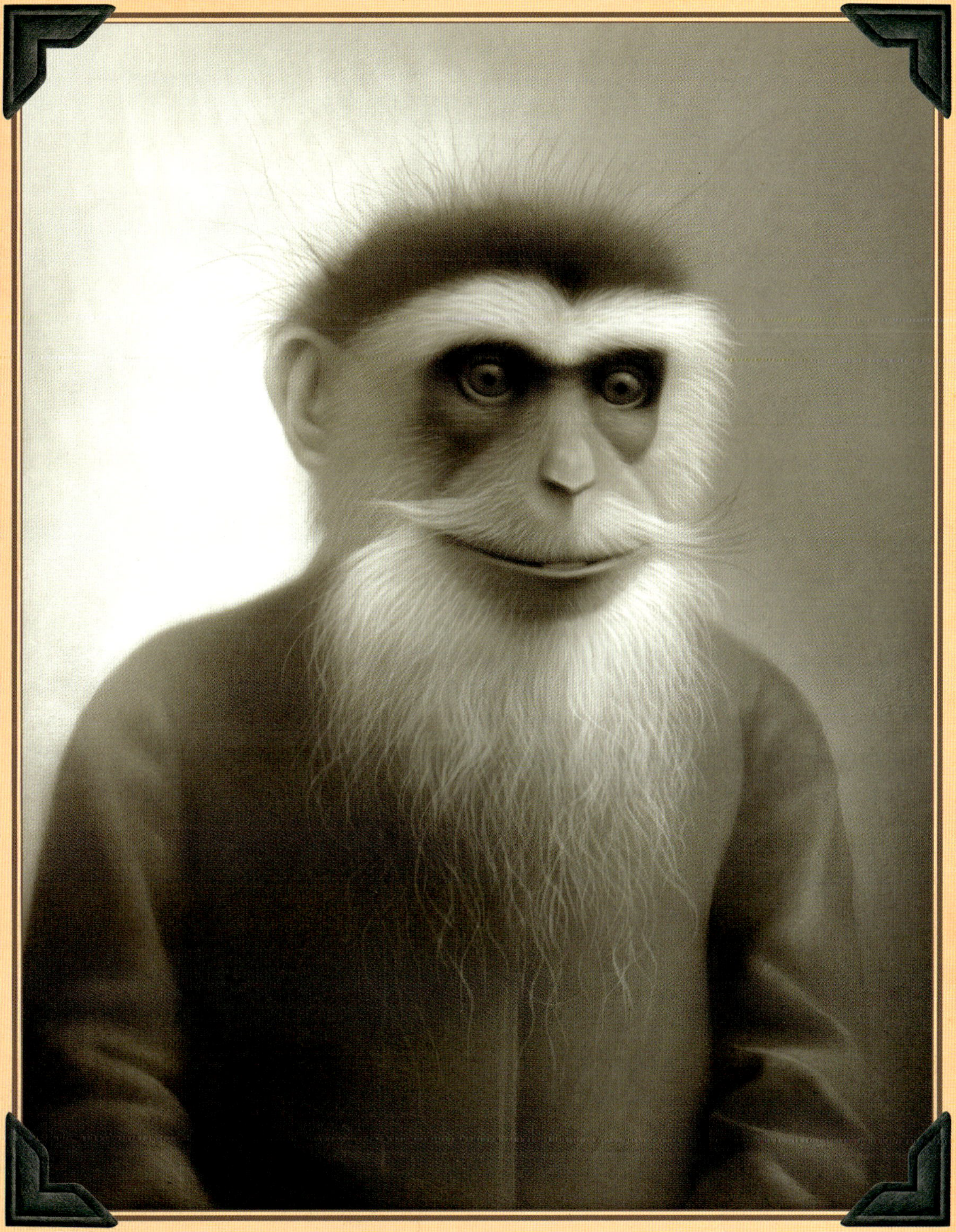

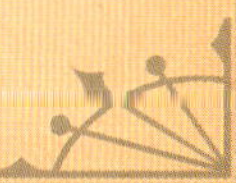

~ MARTIN GIBBON ~

Herbert was a very peculiar simian. He walked upright with a cane and had an unusual gait that consisted of a slow step, followed by a slightly faster one, and then a short hop. His prehensile tail was longer than usual and he used it to pick people's pockets. He did not intend to rob them. He only wanted to find out as much information as he could about them . . . for he loved people. They fascinated him.

Most of his early life was spent working for an organ grinder in a town square in Sheffield. It was his favorite vocation because he was in contact with so many different people. He danced to the sounds of the organ grinder for five years and then, tragically, his employer was run over by a team of Clydesdale horses. As a result, he developed a phobia of horses and a weakness for single malt Scotch.

In 1915, he enlisted in the military and left Sheffield to fight in the trenches for two years. He returned home after suffering the war wound that accounted for his unusual gait and his need for a cane. No longer able to dance, he was forced to get a job at a distillery.

On his first day of work, he came across a team of draft horses and nearly wet himself. To help him overcome his equine anxieties, his fellow workers came up with an elaborate plan. They dressed up as horses and pranced around him for days. When he was hauled away to the asylum, they all apologized and wished him well. He recovered and spent the rest of his days working for shipbuilders in Glasgow and avoiding horses.

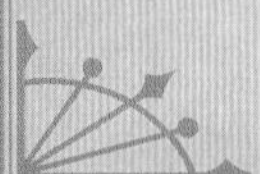

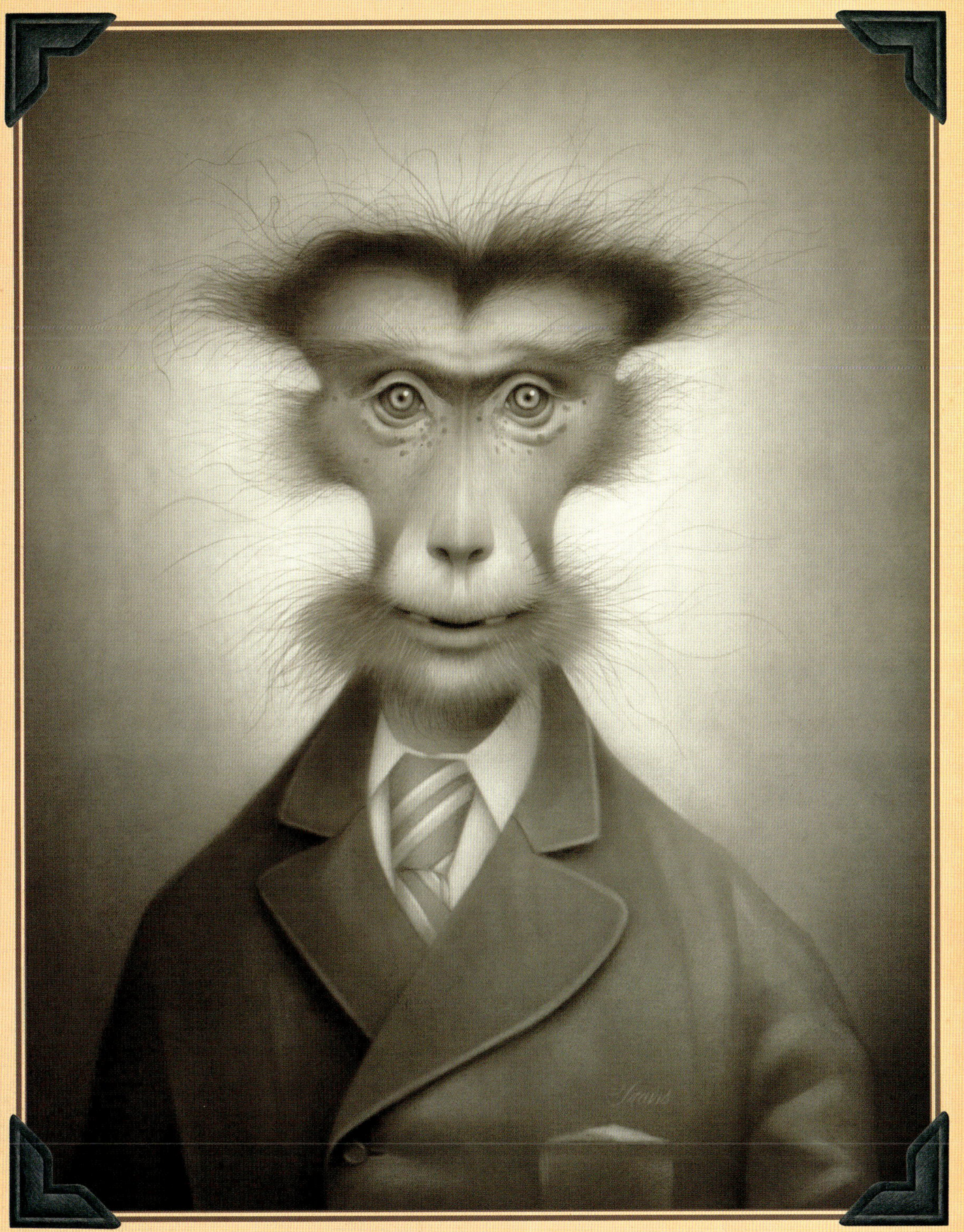

HERBERT

Sluggo came from Chicago and spent years working in the sideshow circuit as a strongman. At 6'11" and 395 pounds, he was quite an imposing figure. The talkers at the carnival shows came up with the idea that Sluggo's mother was frightened by apes at a zoo while she was pregnant with him. No one knew for sure what his true origins were. He was adopted from a workhouse when he was a small boy.

When the sideshows slowed down, he ended up working as a bouncer for a few speakeasies. Because of his formidable appearance, there weren't too many troublemakers. But when there were, he was quite theatrical as he went about his business. He would grab rascals by the shoulders and throw them out with such force that they would land several yards away. There was an awkward grace to their flight patterns, like bags of wet laundry tumbling effortlessly in the air, landing with a thud. After a few fatalities, Sluggo went back to working the sideshows. He eventually retired in Florida.

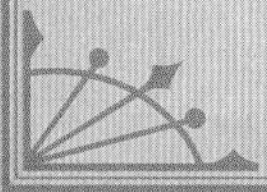

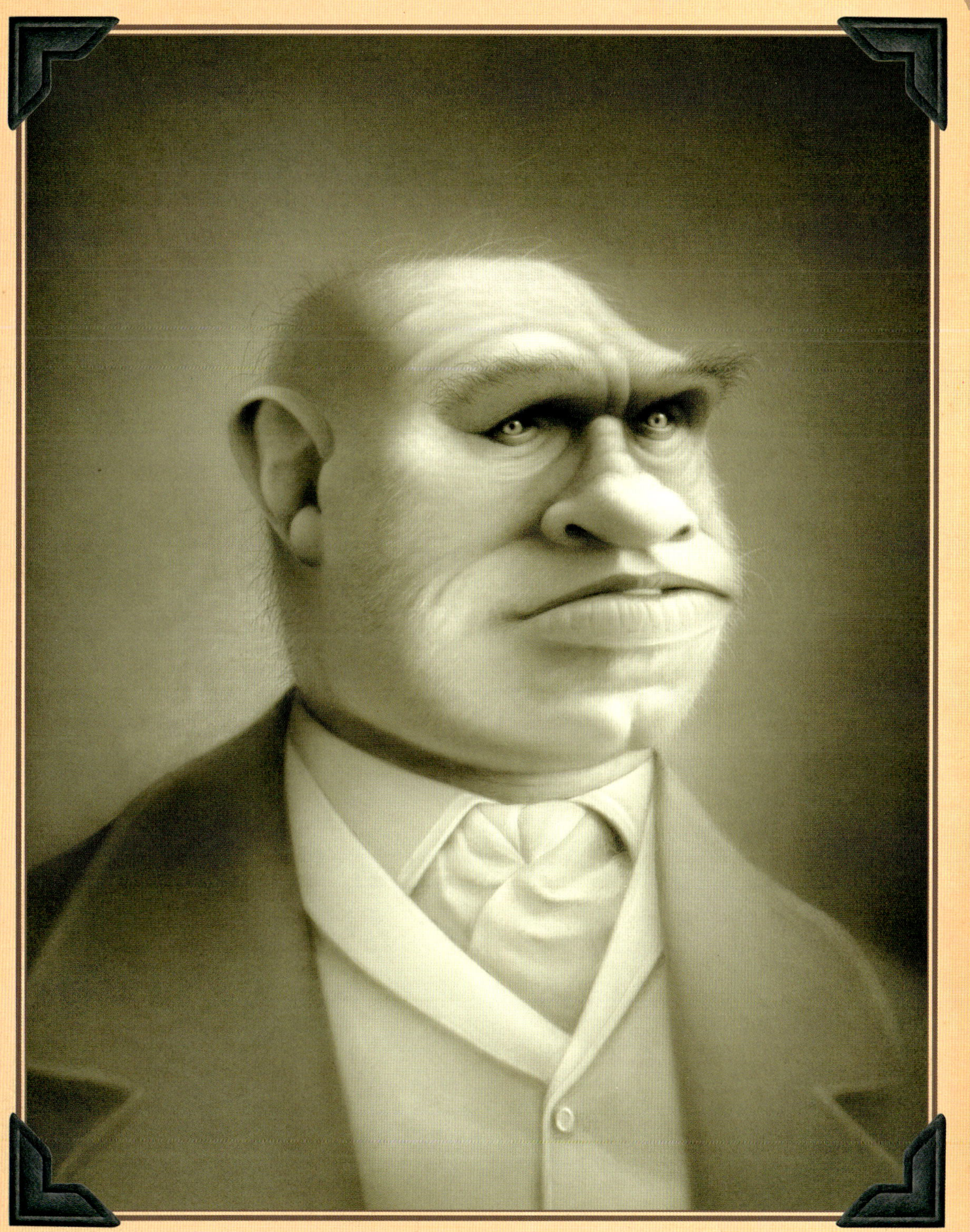

- SLUGGO, THE BIG, BIG MONKEY MAN -

Martin "Squeaky" Parsons lived in a constant state of panic.

He wandered around Kingston, New York, in the 1890s with an expression on his face somewhere between despair and remorse. He had an unusually high, squeaky voice that sounded much like rusty screws being extracted from dry wood panels. Someone once asked him how his day was going, and he threw his arms up and let out a scream that shattered many shop windows. No one knew where he lived and attempts to follow him home were unsuccessful.

Apart from the occasional glass-breaking screeches, he was quite harmless to the public. The local authorities posted signs throughout town explaining how "not to talk to Squeaky." At the start of the First World War, he disappeared. Local veterans of the war claimed to have heard his screams from the trenches.

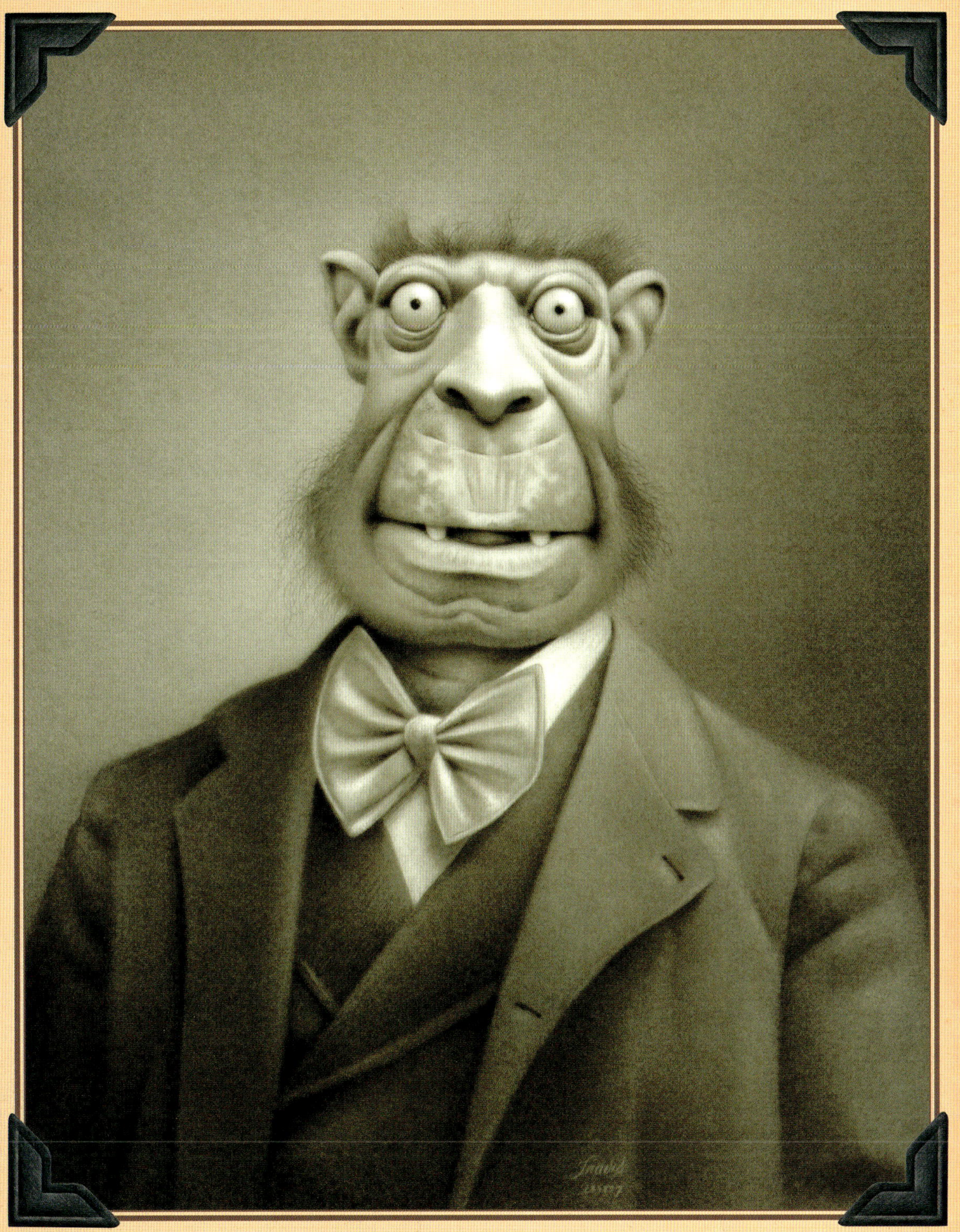

⊷ SQUEAKY ⊶

Big Feet left Ireland in 1859. He was trying to find his brother, who came down with a case of "gold fever" in Northern California. He lost his eye in a fight with some drunken prospectors who mistook him for the legendary "Bigfoot." While he never did find his brother, he managed to find quite a bit of gold along the way.

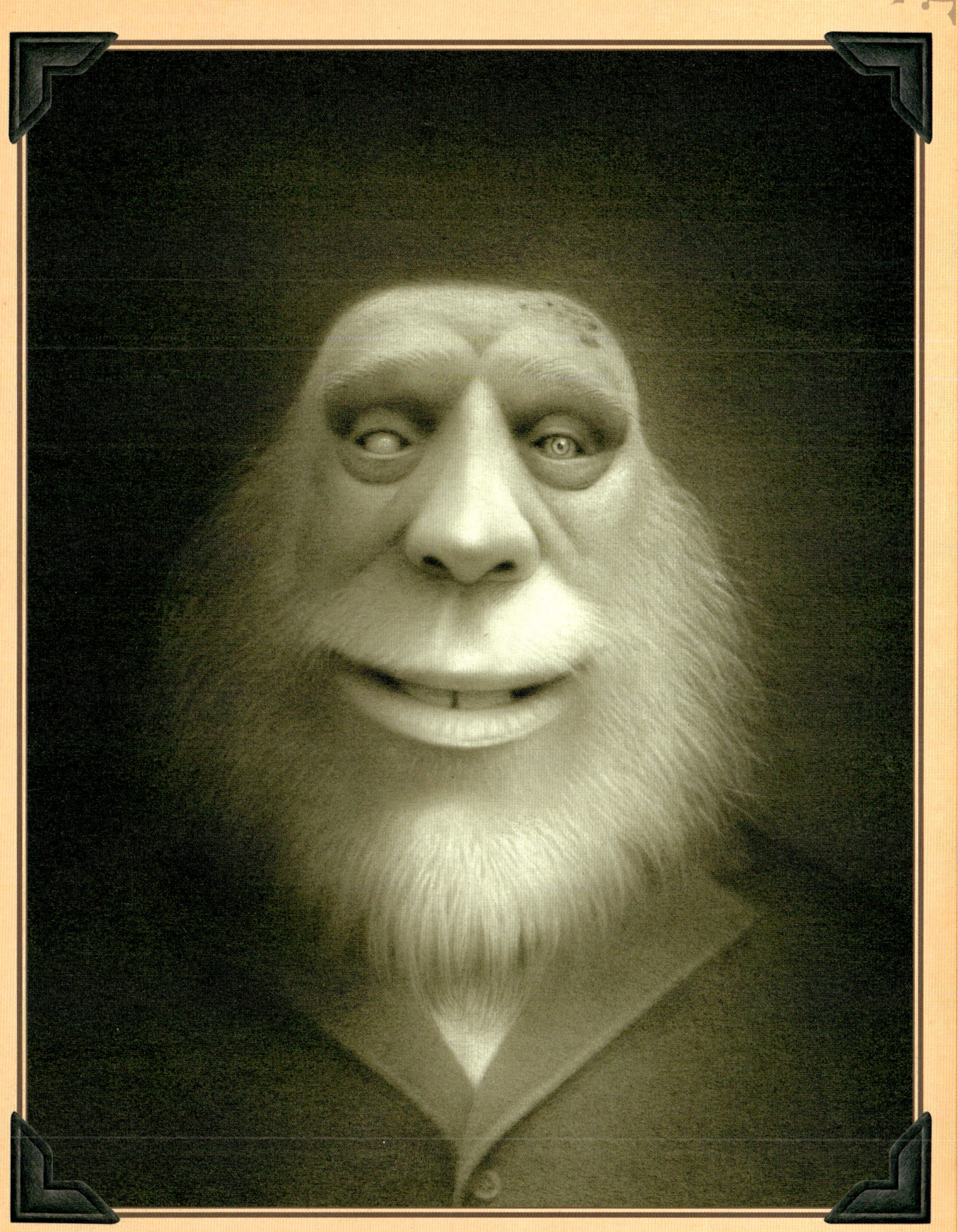

Big Feet

REGINALD COULD HOLD HIS BREATH FOR OVER AN HOUR AND CRACK OPEN OYSTER shells on his chest. He loved eating catfish and preferred single malt Scotch. He had an unusual gait—his arms flailed a bit and he shuffled his feet like an unbalanced penguin. Despite his repulsive body odor, he was the most popular professor during his tenure at Cambridge. His inventions and discoveries garnered him great fame, great wealth, and a knighthood. Always good for a laugh, he was constantly surrounded by women and rarely slept alone. This bristle-faced lothario was the envy of the entire continent. The English catch-phrase for having a good time became "Who's having the life of Reggie now?"

His entire adult life seemed to be one great moment after another. He laughed and laughed . . . invented and achieved . . . and laughed . . . and continued to accomplish seemingly impossible tasks . . . while having possibly the best time that anyone had ever had in the entire history of the world! One good time led to another . . . and another . . . and another, still. Until one day, Sir Reginald dropped his timepiece and when he bent down to retrieve it, he spontaneously combusted! All that remained recognizable on his pile of ashes were his whiskers and his shoes.

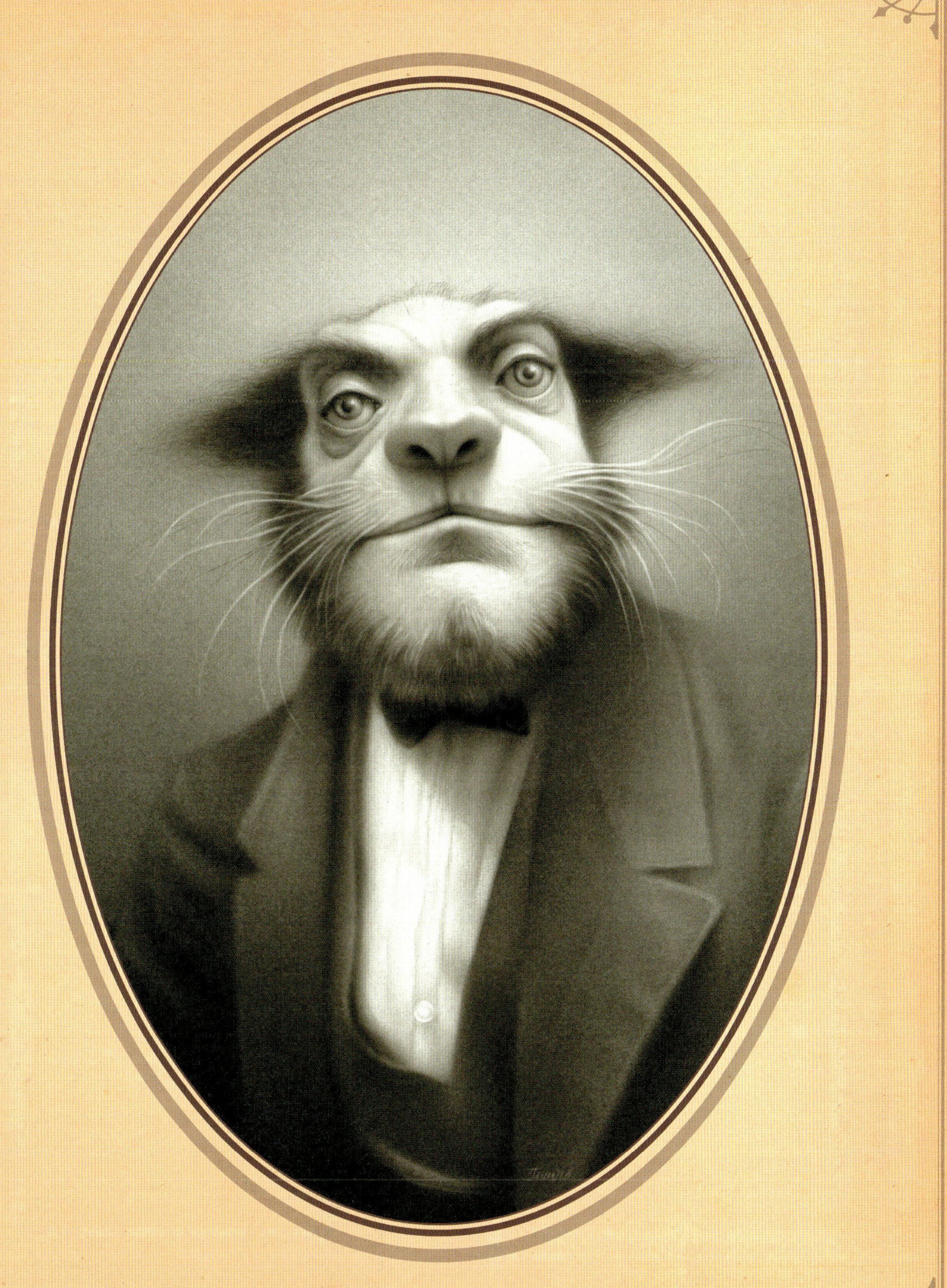

Reginald Whiskers McFerson

His real name was Yuri Medvedev. He was discovered working in a coal mine in Siberia sometime in the 1850s. After being drafted by a traveling circus to be its strongman, his colossal 8'9" frame caught the eye of P. T. Barnum. Barnum wanted to purchase his contract with the intention of exhibiting him in his New York museum of curiosities.

As soon as he arrived in Brooklyn, Yuri balked at the prospect of making a living as a human oddity. He preferred to work with his hands again and took jobs in construction. His formidable size and menacing stare did not go unnoticed. He eventually ended up working as an enforcer for his local union, fighting off strike-breakers.

He survived many attempts on his life. He'd been shot at, had a piano dropped on him, been pushed off the Brooklyn Bridge and was even ambushed by brick-throwers, which earned him his nickname, "Bricktop."

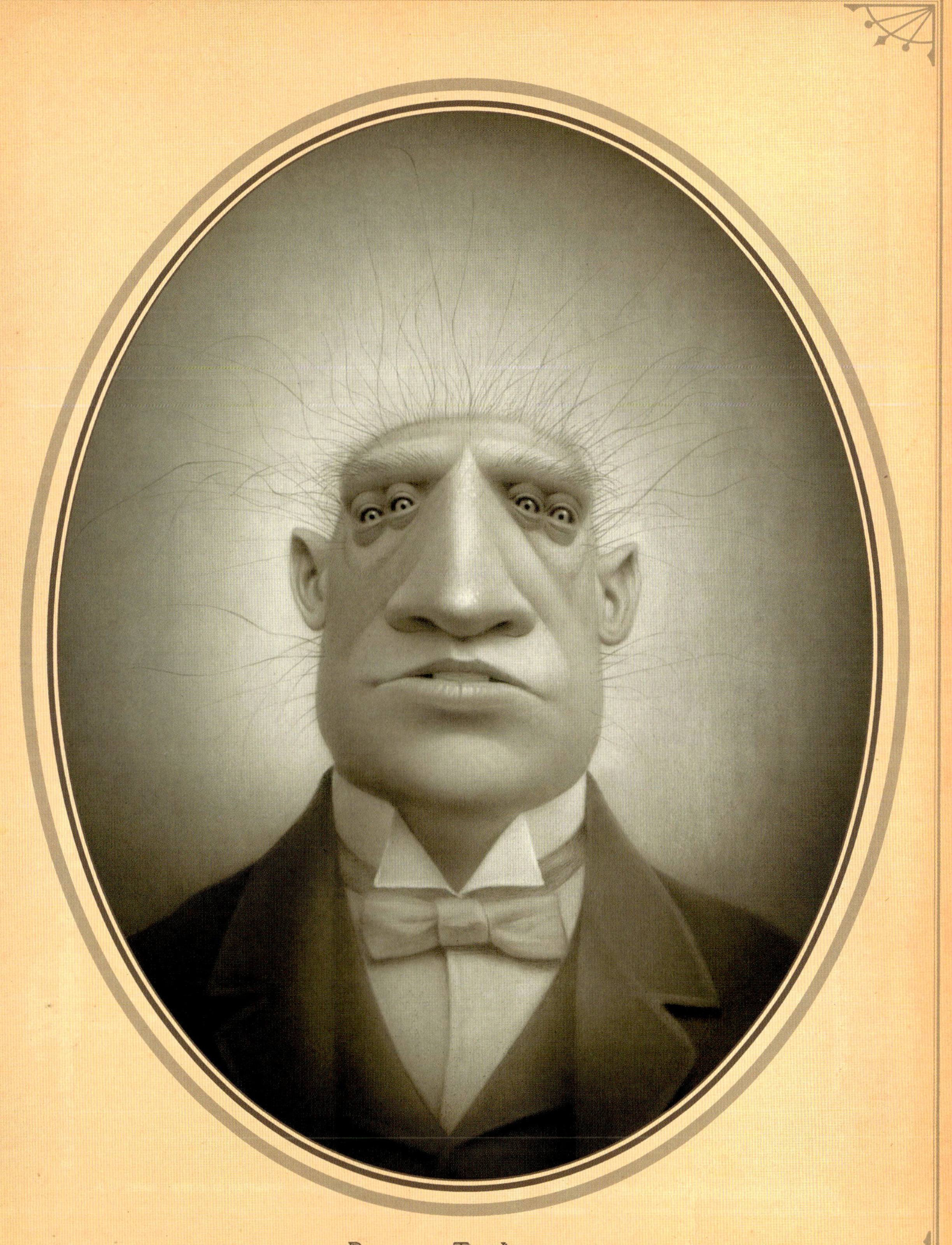

BRICKTOP, THE LUMMOX

I N 1923 A MAN NAMED M AX DISCOVERED THAT HIS DOG, C HARLIE, HAD GONE
through his closets while he was working at the bank. Sometimes he came
home to find Charlie wearing his clothes or sitting in his favorite chair with
a pipe in his mouth. A month later, Charlie began walking upright and
used his front paws to make gestures while he barked. Even more disturbing,
while Max was unlocking the front door, he thought he saw Charlie talking
to someone. One day, Charlie greeted Max at the door with a cigar in his
mouth and told him he would explain everything. He then asked Max for a
small loan to cover some expenses.

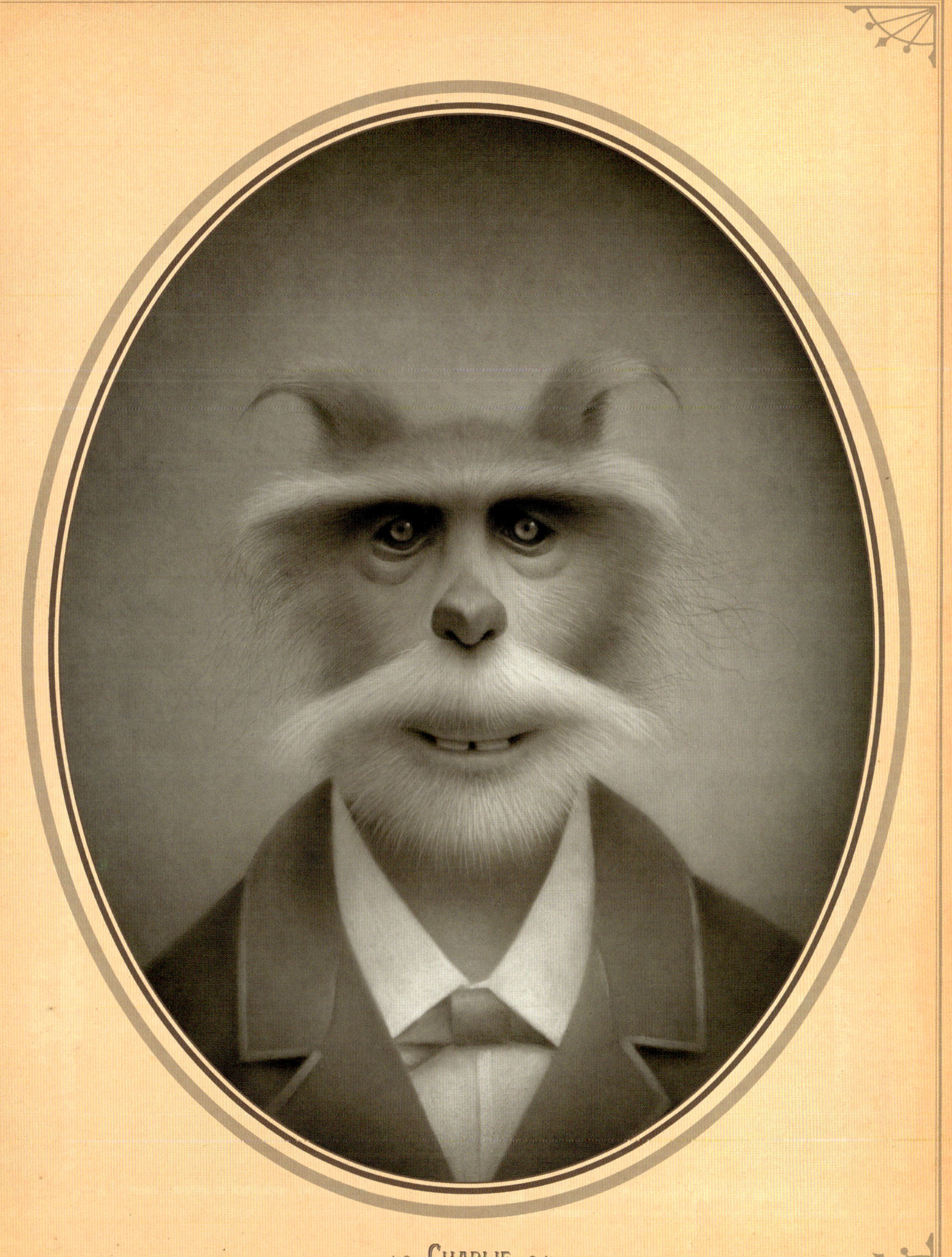

CHARLIE

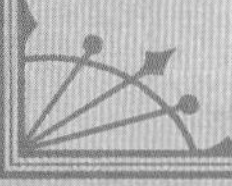

One cold November night, two friends lost a bet.

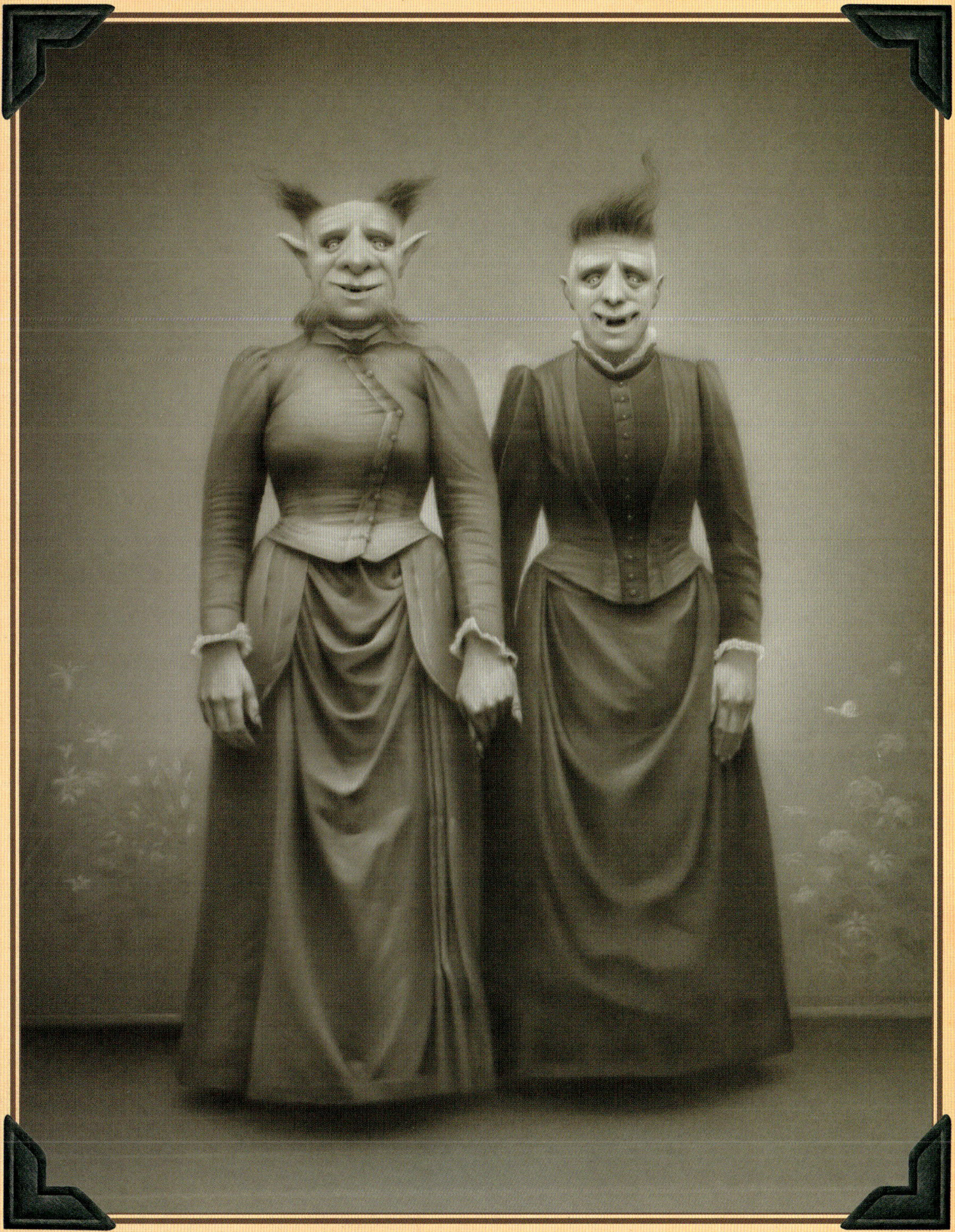

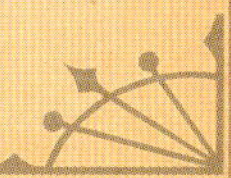

PALS

It was said that Charlotte Stilton ran off into the woods after an argument with her husband and never came home. Twenty-five years later, locals claimed that her ghost roamed the forest and that her apparition could be seen planting new trees every spring.

To this day, no one hunts in those woods for fear of catching "Stilton's Revenge." It is said that she makes it very difficult for hunters. She curses them with stomach ailments, bouts of memory loss, and the tendency to be accident prone. There have been many reports of people shooting themselves in the foot and vomiting. She is also said to be kind, helping people find their way when they are lost in her woods.

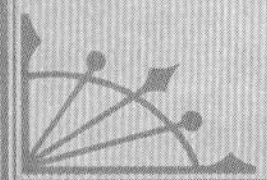

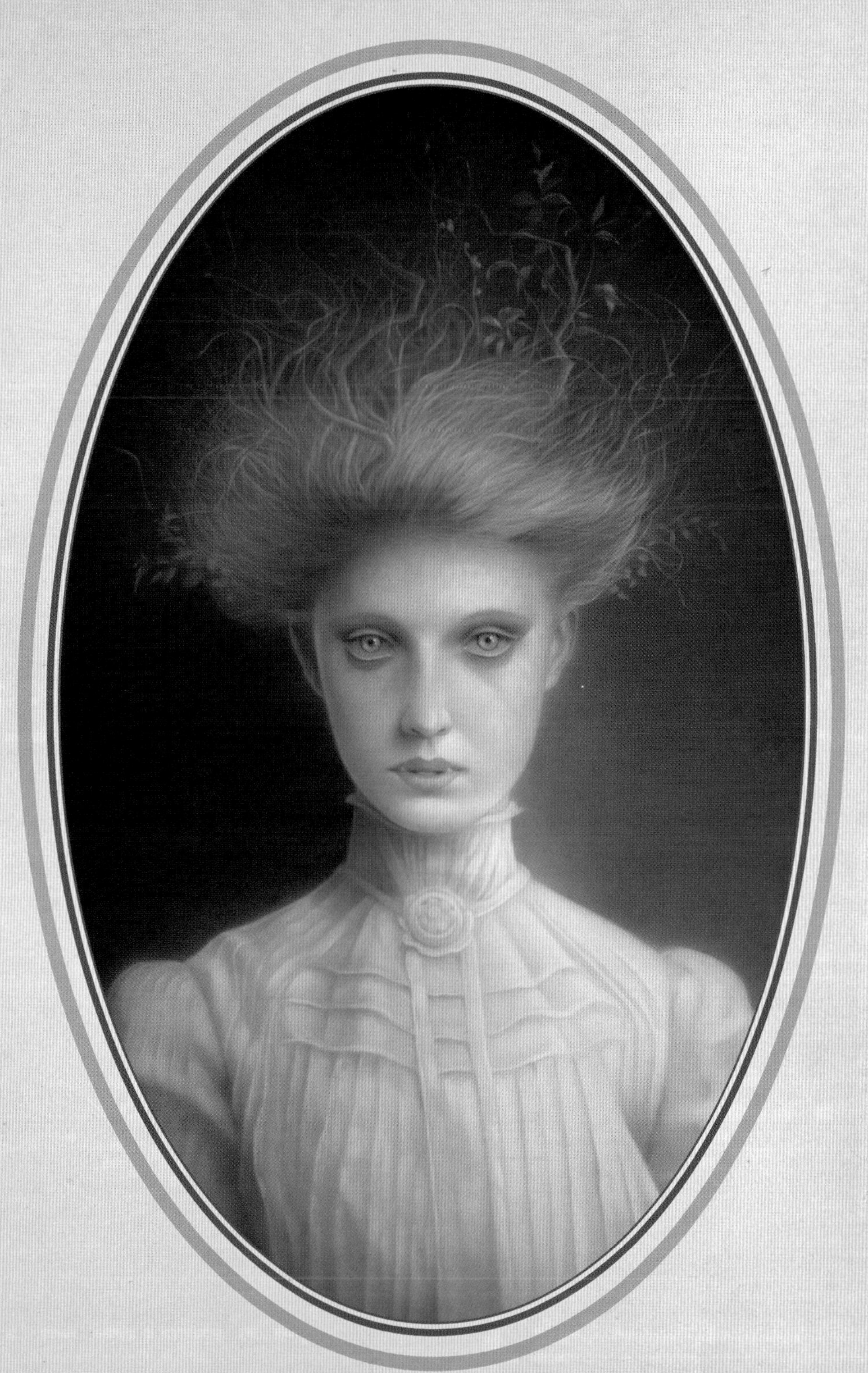

- ❧ Forest Nymph ☙ -

Frank lived on the third floor and spent most of his spare time pacing back and forth in the hallway. When his pacing was interrupted by other tenants trying to get to their rooms, he stopped and stared at them—sometimes following them—offering spare change and free advice about how to properly pace back and forth. At about noon on Thursdays, he would drop to the ground and press his ear to the floor. After about twenty seconds, he would rise to his feet and walk down to the second floor. When he returned to his hallway, he always had a fresh white flower pinned to his jacket.

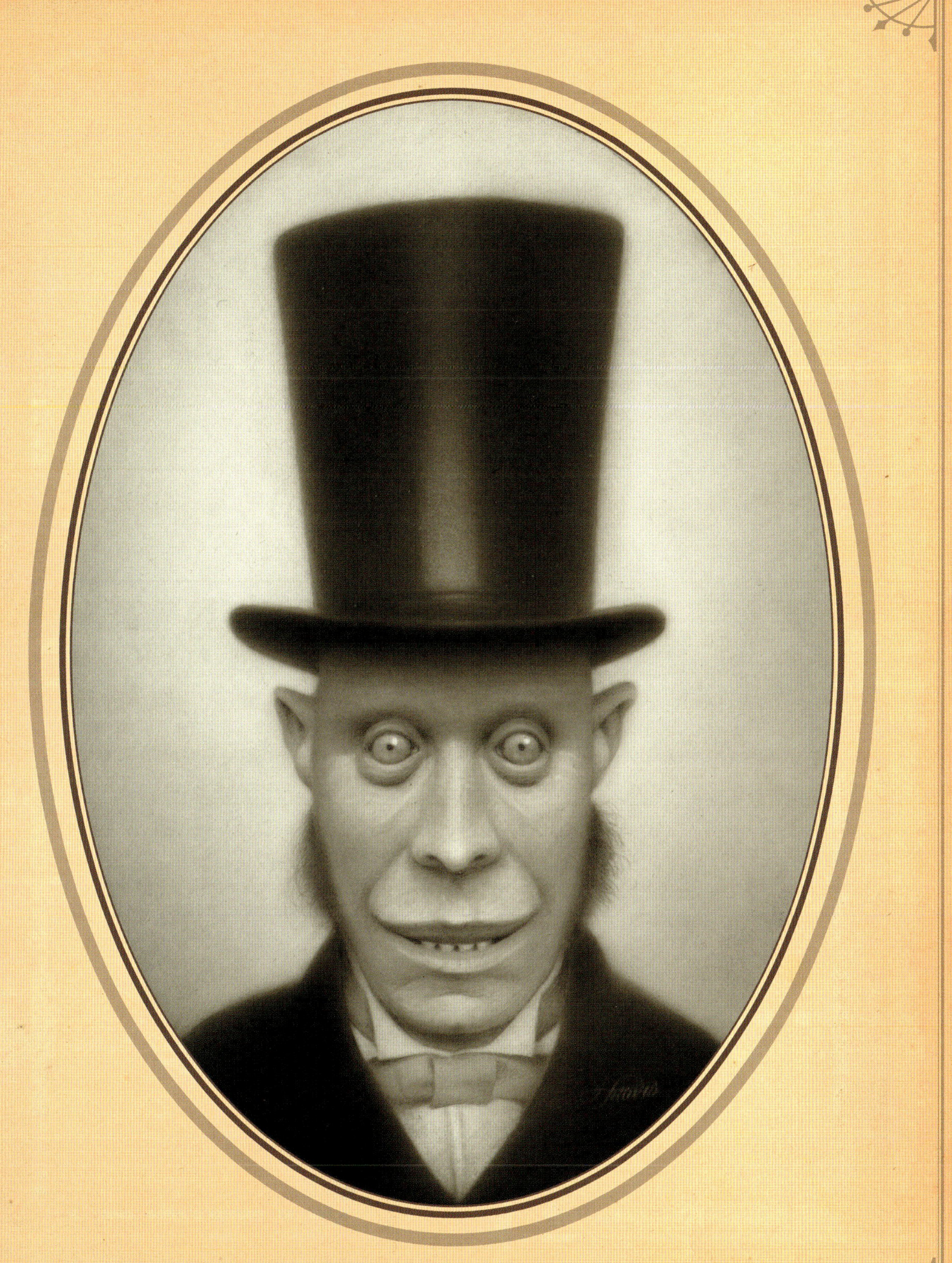

⤞ ❖ ⤝   FRANK THE GAWKER   ⤞ ❖ ⤝

George was a formidable bare knuckles boxer. His oversized chin was as hard as granite and he was difficult to hit. But the most astonishing thing about facing him in a match was the way he flapped his big lips while he boxed. It sounded like a flock of seagulls in full flight. As his lips flapped, every so often, a bubble would form and float out of his mouth like a child's lost balloon. If that wasn't distracting enough, he would begin telling jokes and laughing loudly at all the punch lines. All the while, he pummeled his opponents into submission.

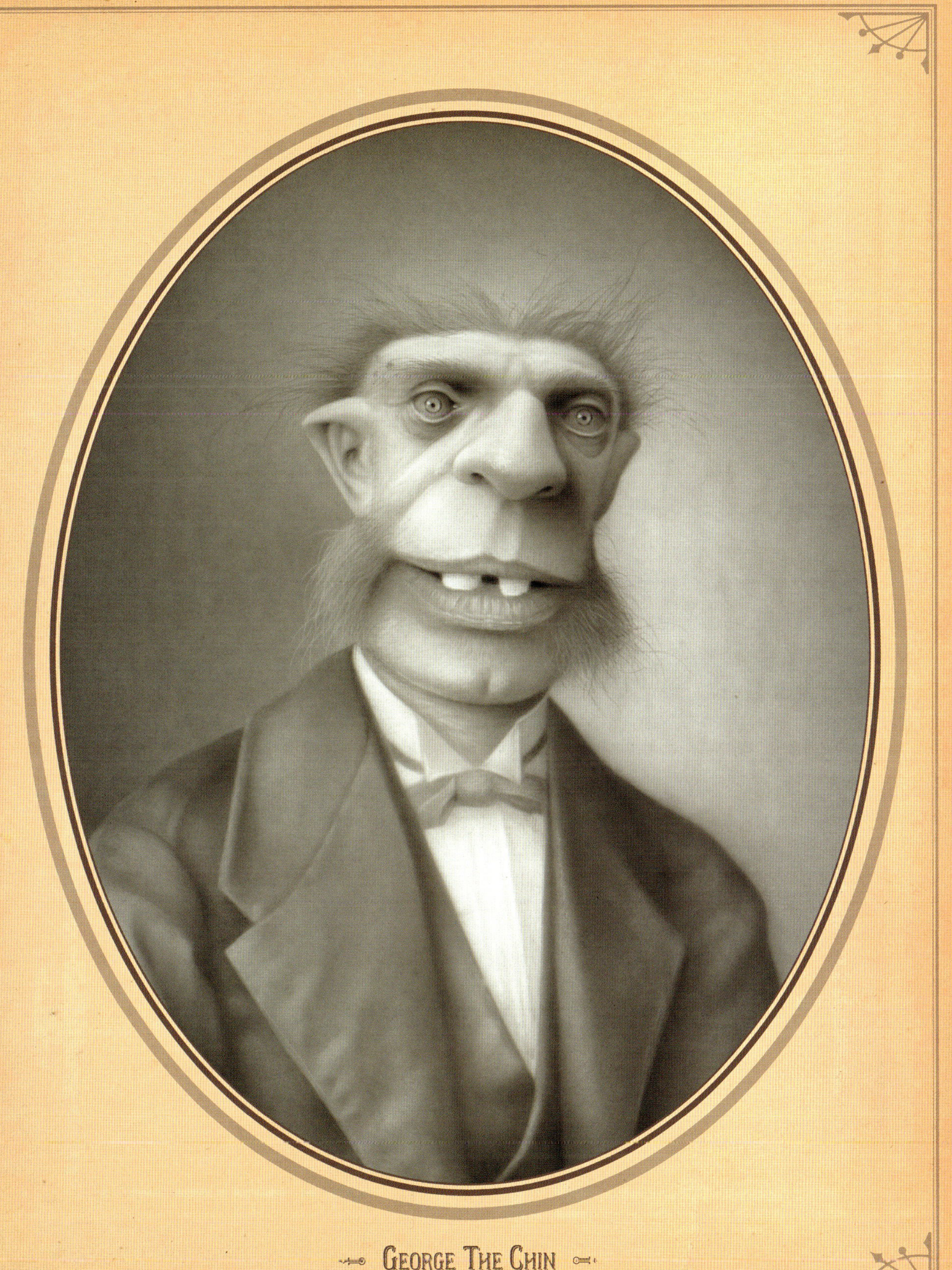

George The Chin

A day before the opening of the 1939 World's Fair, Gill pulled himself out of the great Flushing Bay and headed toward Main Street. After eating a hot dog and a strawberry ice cream soda, he went back into the bay. He reappeared many decades later in the upper deck of Shea Stadium during the 1986 World Series between the New York Mets and the Boston Red Sox. He was enjoying a hot dog and a beer.

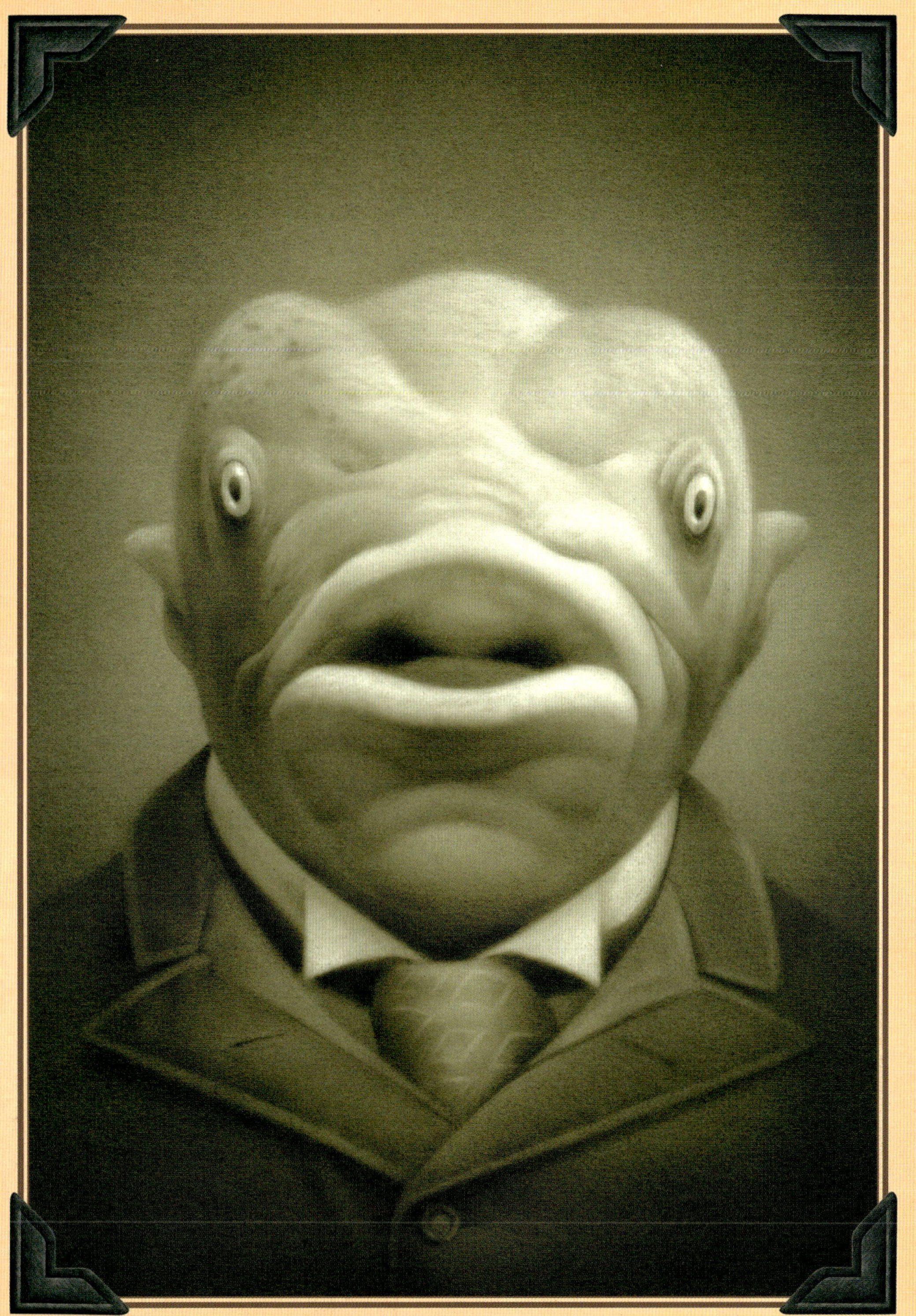

GILL

In 1923, Jonathan "Feelerbrows" decided to retire from his sideshow job as a mystic. When he was in the carnival circuit, it was an uncanny experience to watch him work his act. He would walk out onto the stage and make a quick, mundane prognostication about the weather or the day's sporting events, and then he would ask for silence while he pretended to energize his "mystical powers." He then wiggled his unusually long eyebrows like antennae on an insect. After randomly picking audience members to participate, he would accurately tell a person's fortune; including their weight, favorite color, place of origin, and what they ingested three days prior.

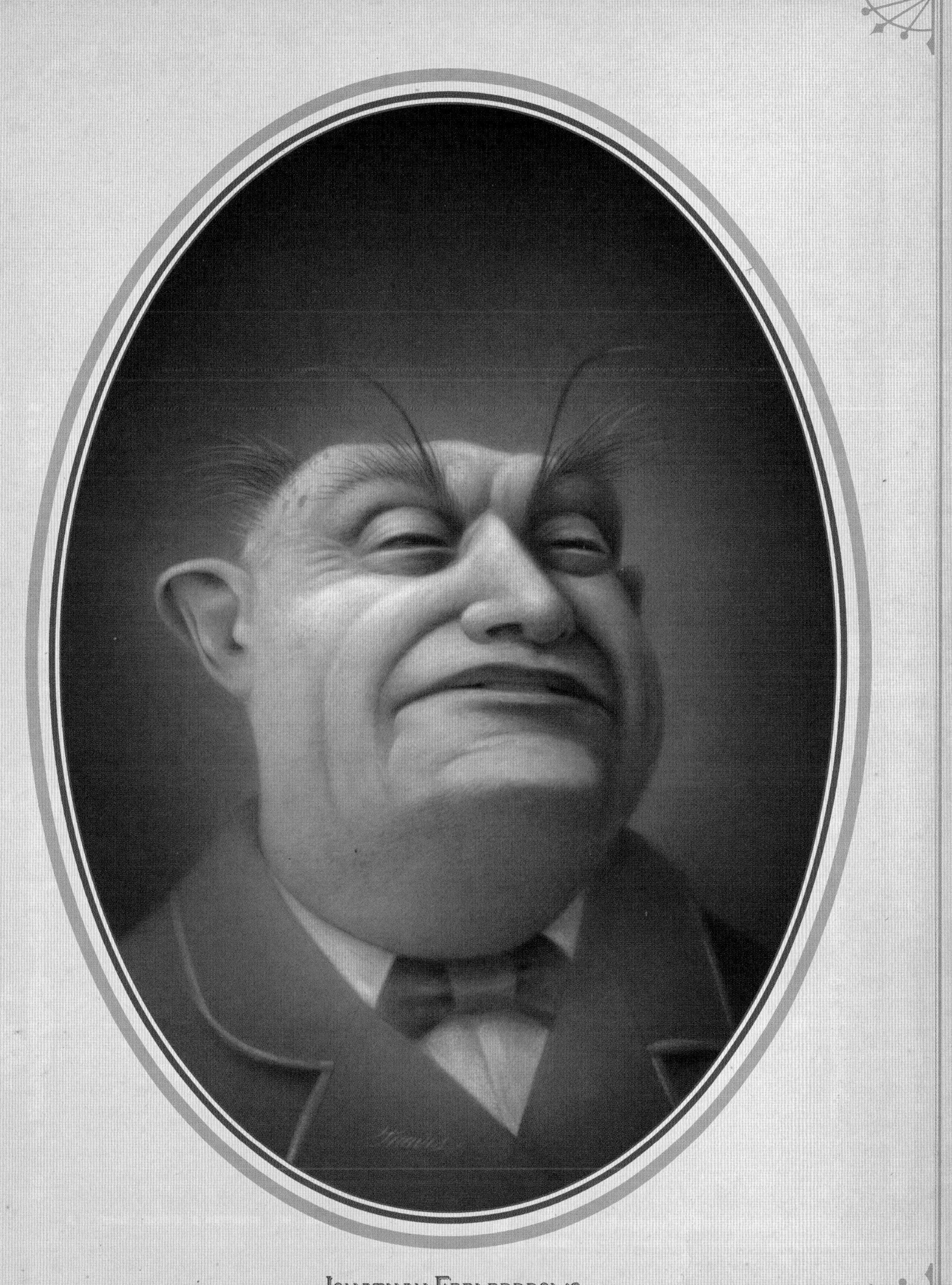

Jonathan Feelerbrows

SOMETIME IN THE LATE 1850S, AFTER AN UNUSUALLY LONG, HARD RAIN, A STRANGE figure pulled himself out of the ground and began terrorizing a small mining town in Northern California. It wasn't so much that he actually, physically hurt anyone . . . it was his unusual appearance combined with his high-pitched cackling and near constant mumbling, which caused a strong vibration that rattled windowpanes and interrupted many a conversation. He was nicknamed "Rooty" because of the long root-like tendrils that protruded from the top of his misshapen head and the strong scent of ginseng that came from his body.

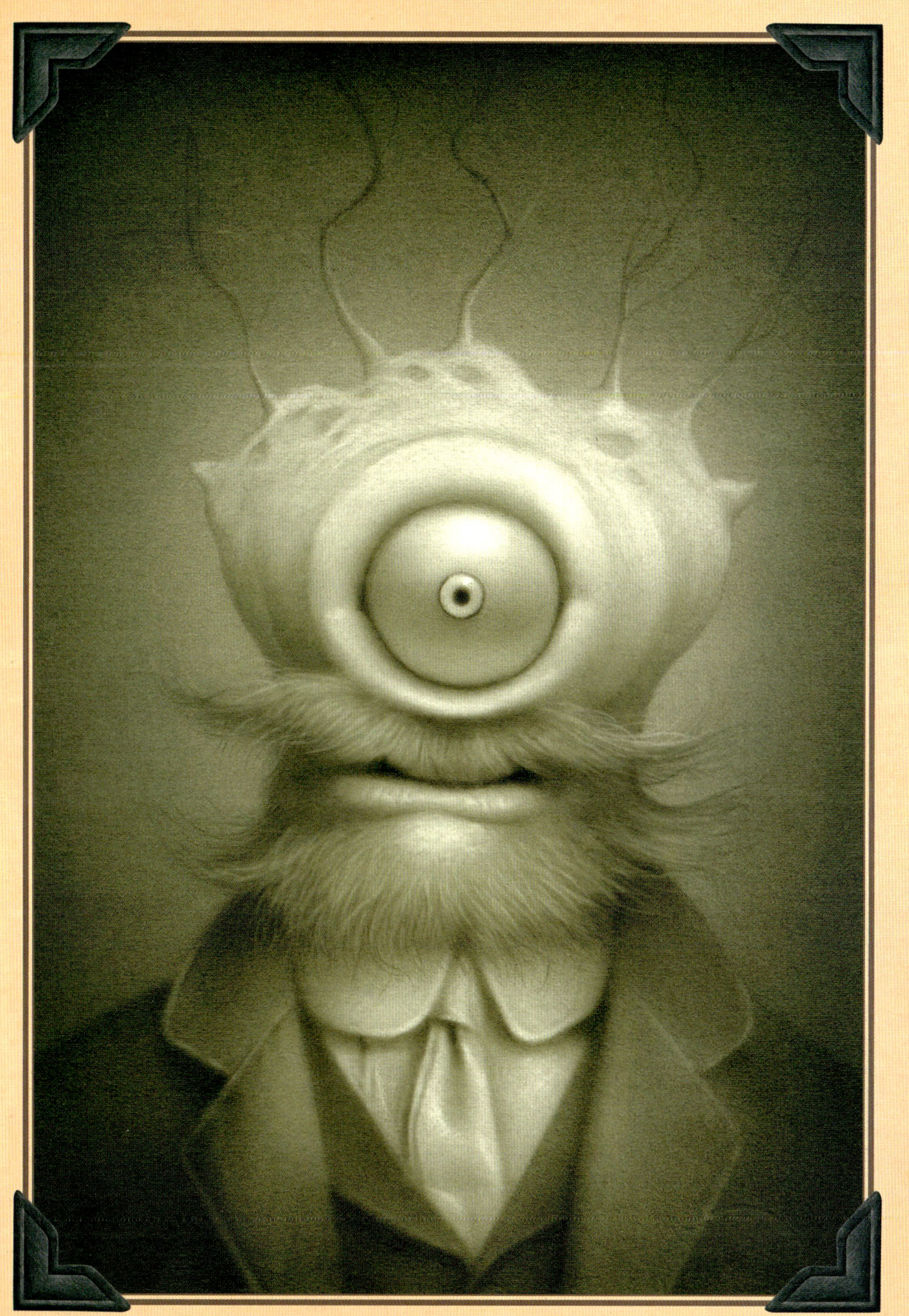

⇥ ROOTY ⇤

STEPHEN WAS A LITTLE-KNOWN COMPETITOR TO NIKOLA TESLA. HE SUFFERED from a severe case of narcolepsy. History essentially has forgotten this great inventor because he was a chronic oversleeper and could never make it to the patent office in time. His great discoveries in electricity and magnetism were legendary.

One autumn evening in 1937, his home began to light up like a Christmas tree. The blinking light attracted a small crowd of curious onlookers who let out a gasp when the house started to levitate off the ground. After a loud pop, the house fell back down and there was a great explosion of light. The force of the blast knocked everyone to the ground. The dark brick home had turned white. After a few seconds, it collapsed into a pile of powder. Stephen was found standing in the middle of the ashes. He appeared normal except for his upright hair and the soft glow that his body emitted for months after the incident.

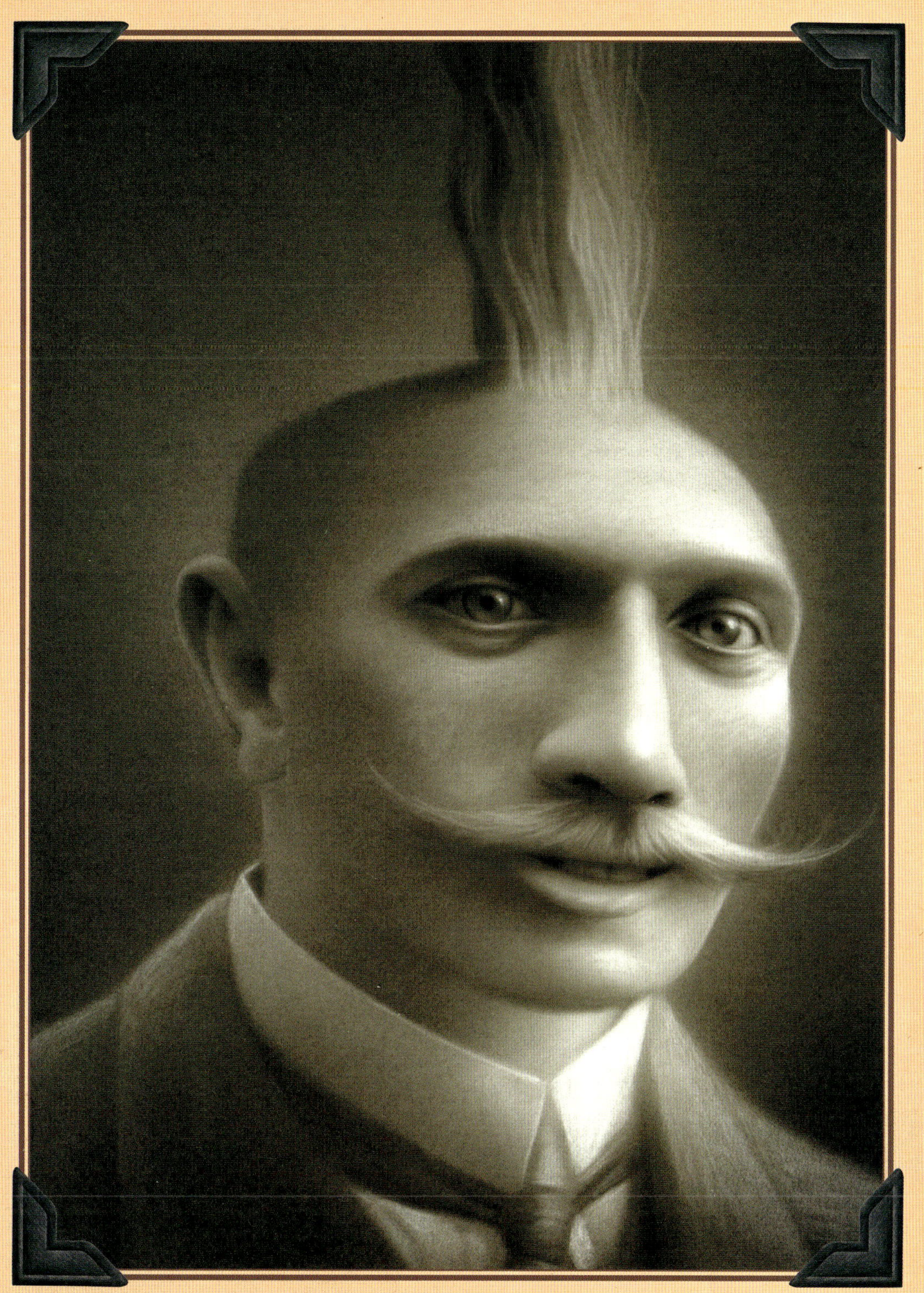

STEPHEN OF UNUSUAL CIRCUMSTANCES

WHEN HE FIRST APPEARED ON THE SIDESHOW CIRCUIT, REX WAS BILLED AS "Rusty, the Wonderdog." He was the world's one and only fire-eating dog. He could also perform amazing feats of strength; he could bend the points of a pitchfork with his jaws! He was last seen working at Coney Island's Dreamland as the "Living Gargoyle" in the Hell Gate exhibition. The park burned down in 1911.

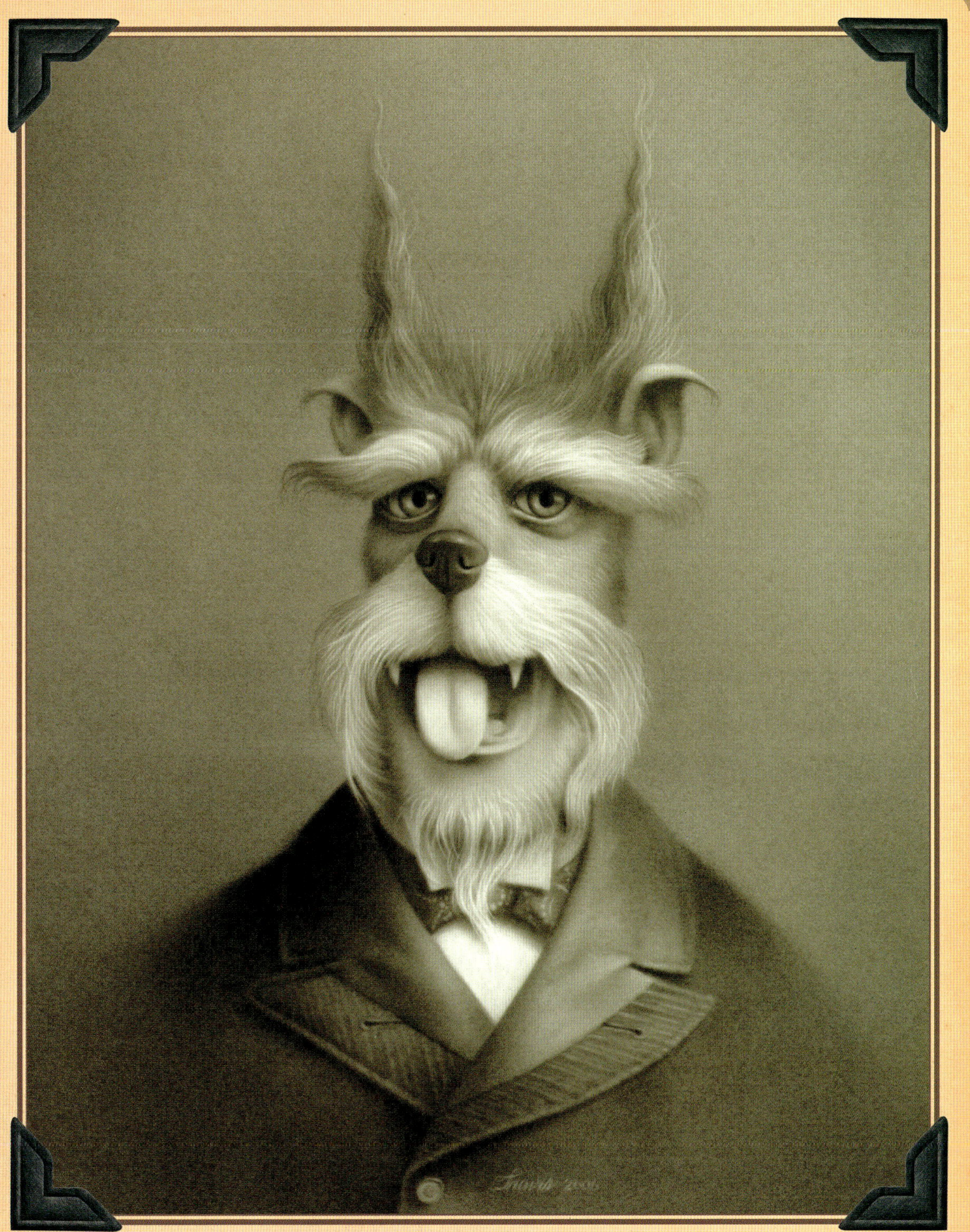

Rex of Unusual Circumstances

Walter was proud of his prodigious teeth. He learned how to grin just to show them off. When there was a strong wind, it made a whistling noise as it passed through his open mouth. Sometimes he would run really fast while holding the grin on his face just to hear the whistling noise.

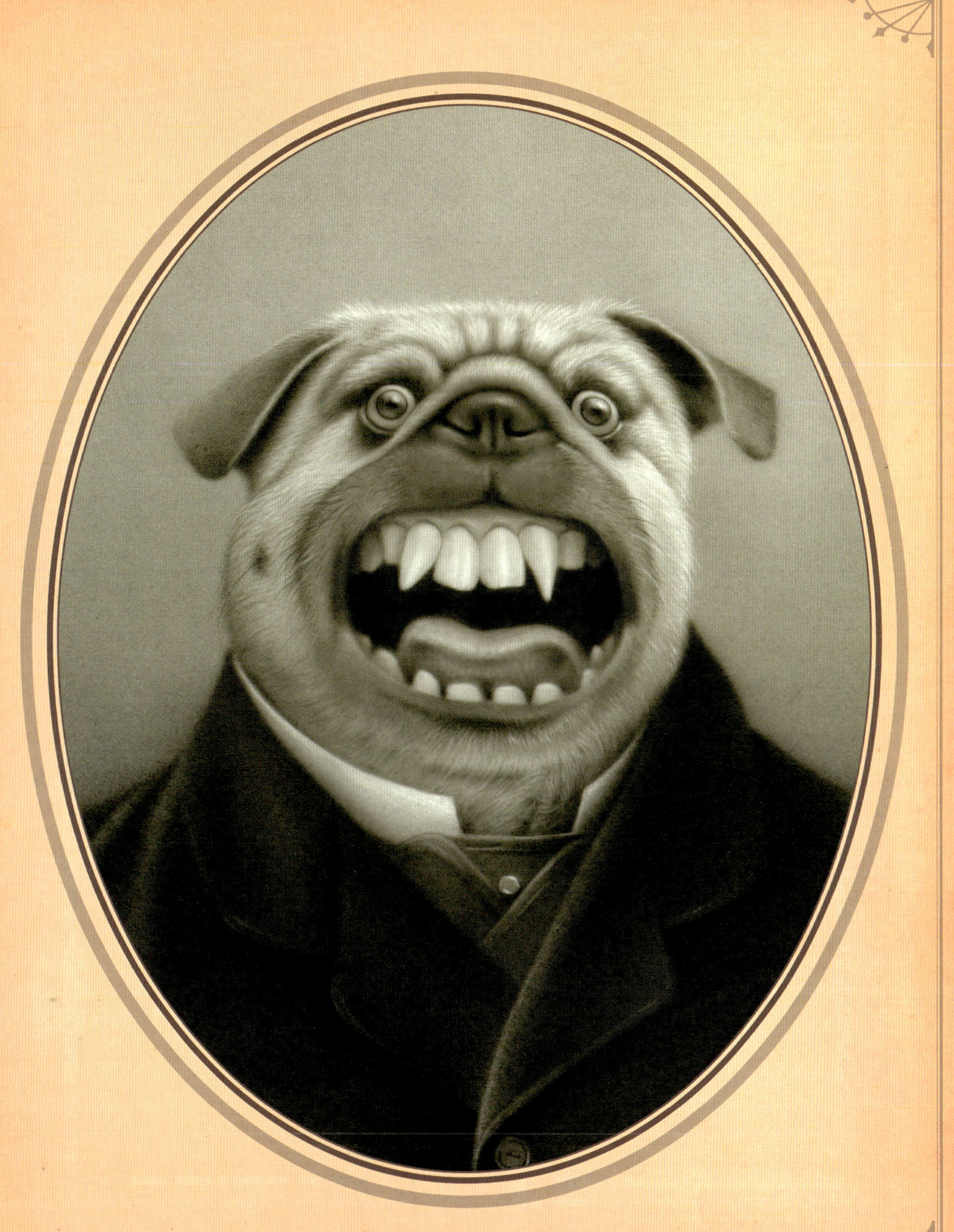

⊷ WALTER PUG ⊶

DANNY LIKED PUMPKINS . . . HE ATE THEM AS OFTEN AS HE COULD. ONE FALL evening, he ate a large discolored one, (it was slightly rotten). When he lay down to sleep, he had the worst nightmares. He dreamed that he had turned into a monster!

He woke up screaming. The dream seemed so real that he had to go to the mirror and look at himself. He gave out a sigh of relief: He still had his award-winning smile, his crooked teeth, and his charming three eyes, (a sign of maturity for the common northeast pumpkin eater). He had a big day ahead of him . . . it was his turn to terrorize the people visiting the pumpkin patch and, of course, to eat as many pumpkins as he could.

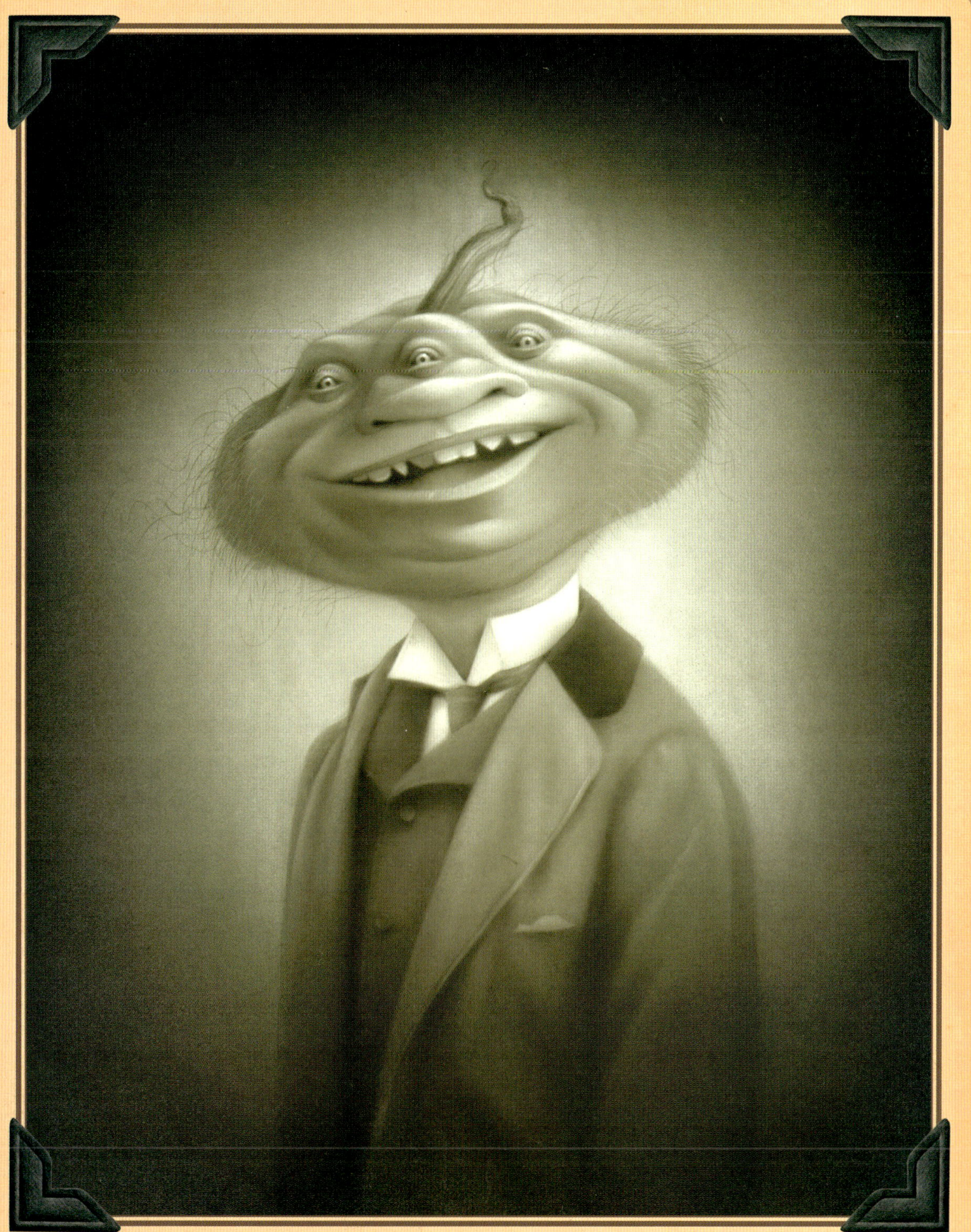

PUMPKIN HEAD

Not much is known about Morley.

He was found sleeping in a hedge outside of Devonshire in 1883. The family that discovered him brought him into their home and let him stay there. He loved gardening and spent evenings working their garden.

After a few weeks of this nightly routine, he disappeared. All that was found was a large hole in the middle of the garden that was an opening to a tunnel that seemed to go for miles underground.

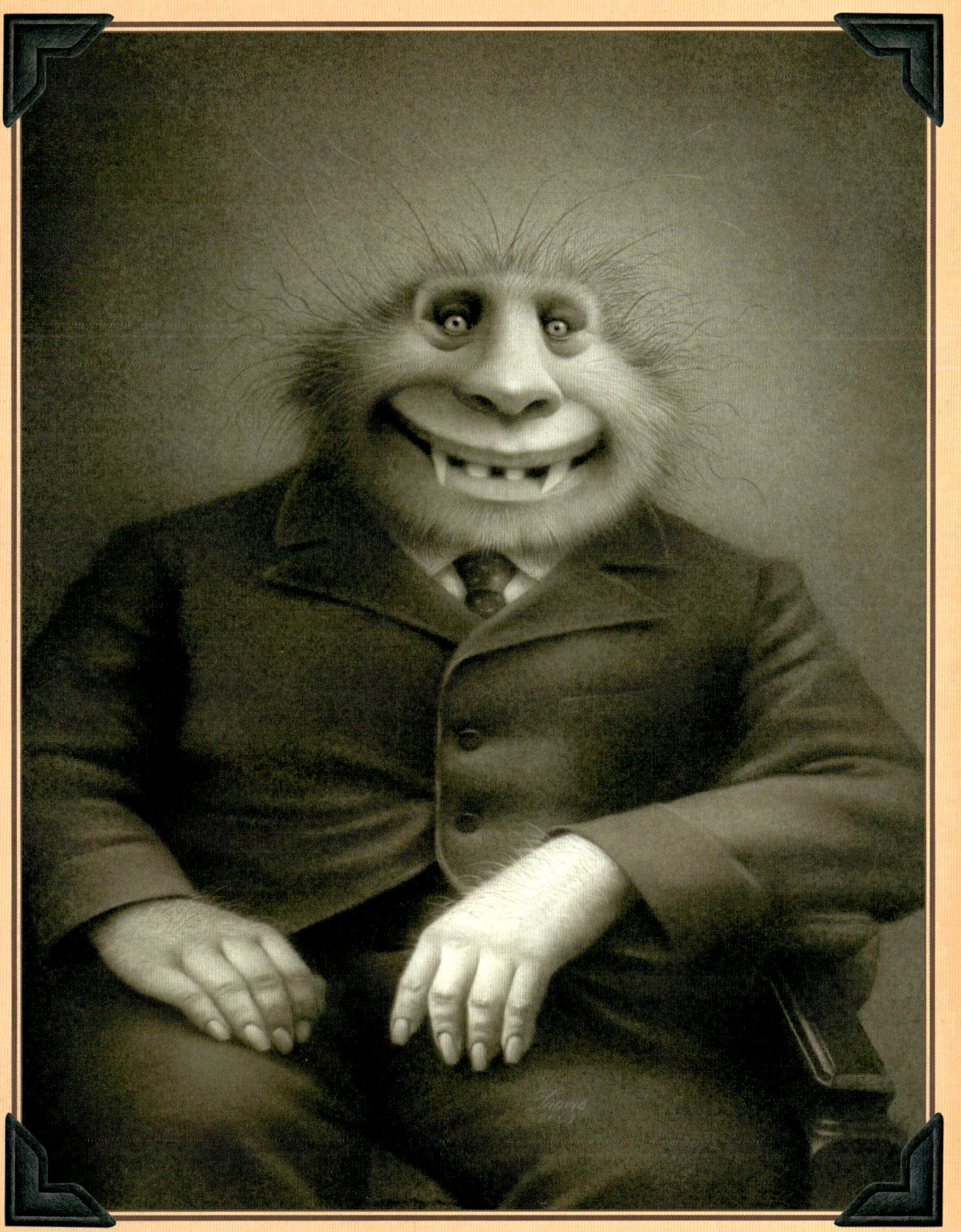

— **Morley Hedge** —

In 1894, Mortimer T. Blaschfeld had an awful itch. It turned out to be lice, and he promptly had his head shaved. After discovering his oddly shaped pate, he gave up his job as a tailor and decided he could earn more money as a sideshow exhibit. He was billed as the original "What Is It?" and wore a furry outfit he made from scraps. He worked at Coney Island's Dreamland until the park burned down.

He took the fiery disaster as a sign to return to his original profession. He managed to save his costume from the blaze and wore it one more time as a practical joke. Unfortunately, he was shot down in a hail of gunfire by off-duty police officers.

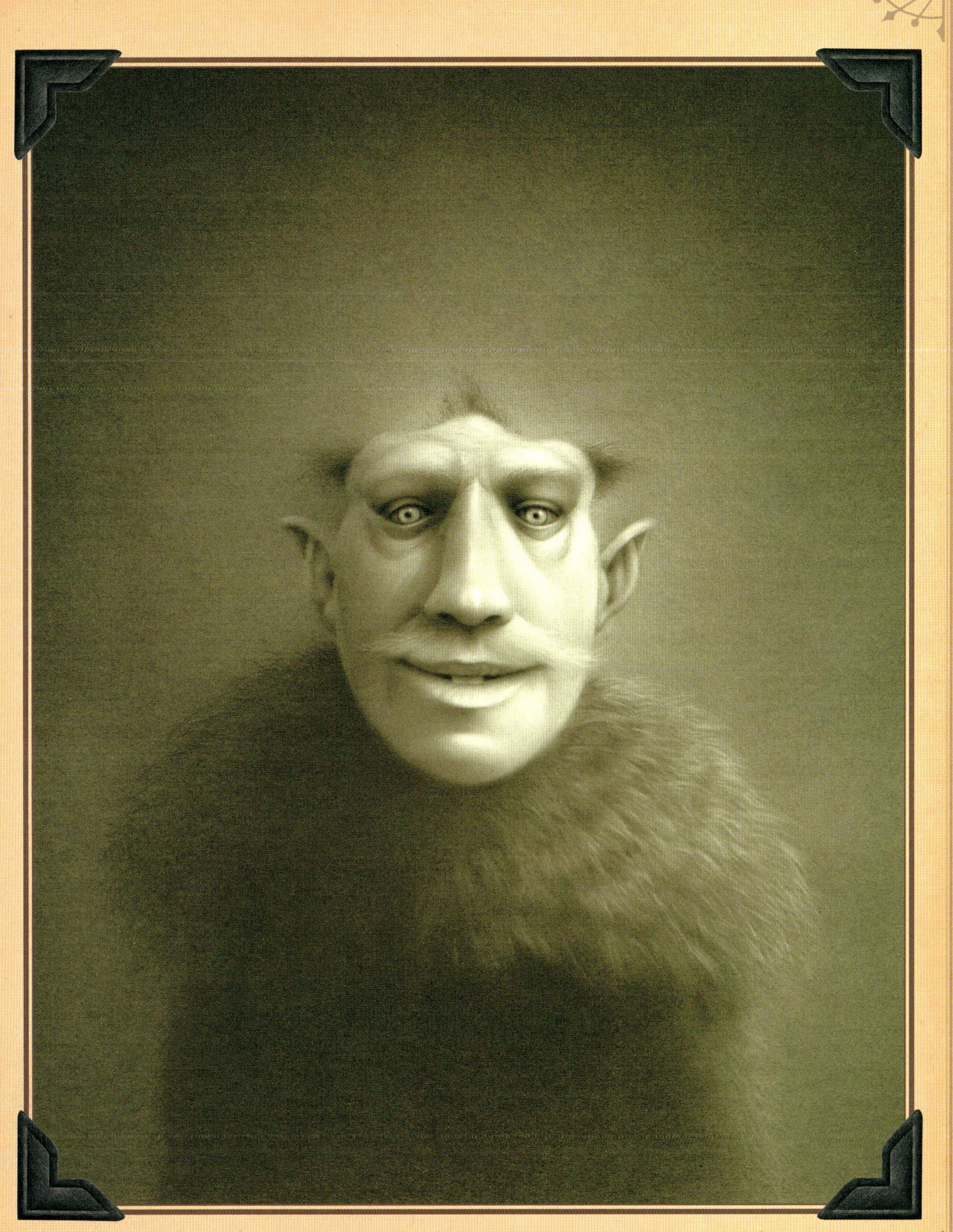

MORT AT LUNA PARK

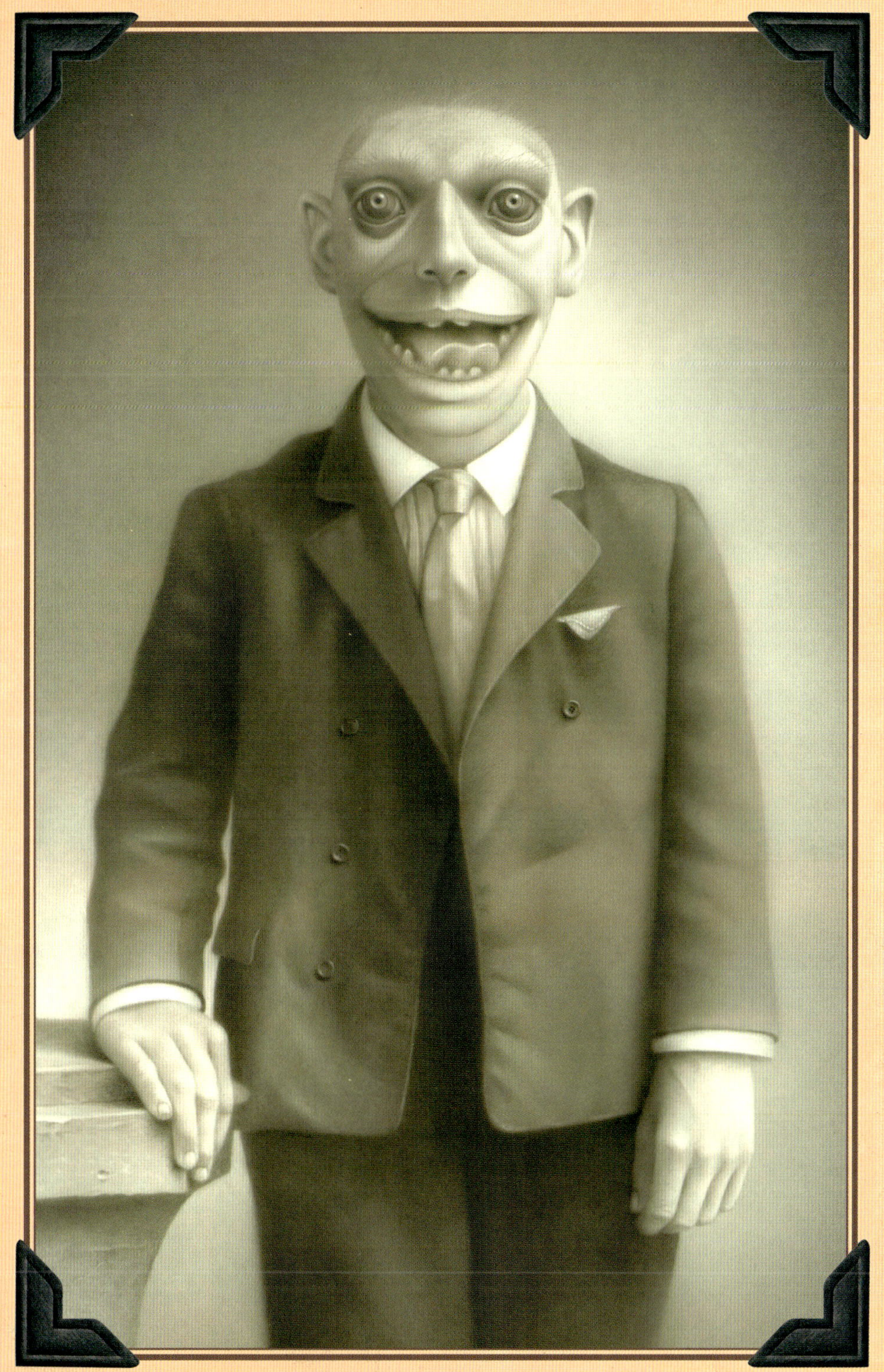

— ❖ — MR. ENTHUSIASM — ❖ —

Miss Bunny wandered out of the woods near Hastings, in 1893, to look for her family. They were devoured by wild dogs. She was adopted by a wealthy family and was sent to a boarding school. During that time she took up acting and, after graduation, became a popular London stage actress. She retired to a farm in Southern England.

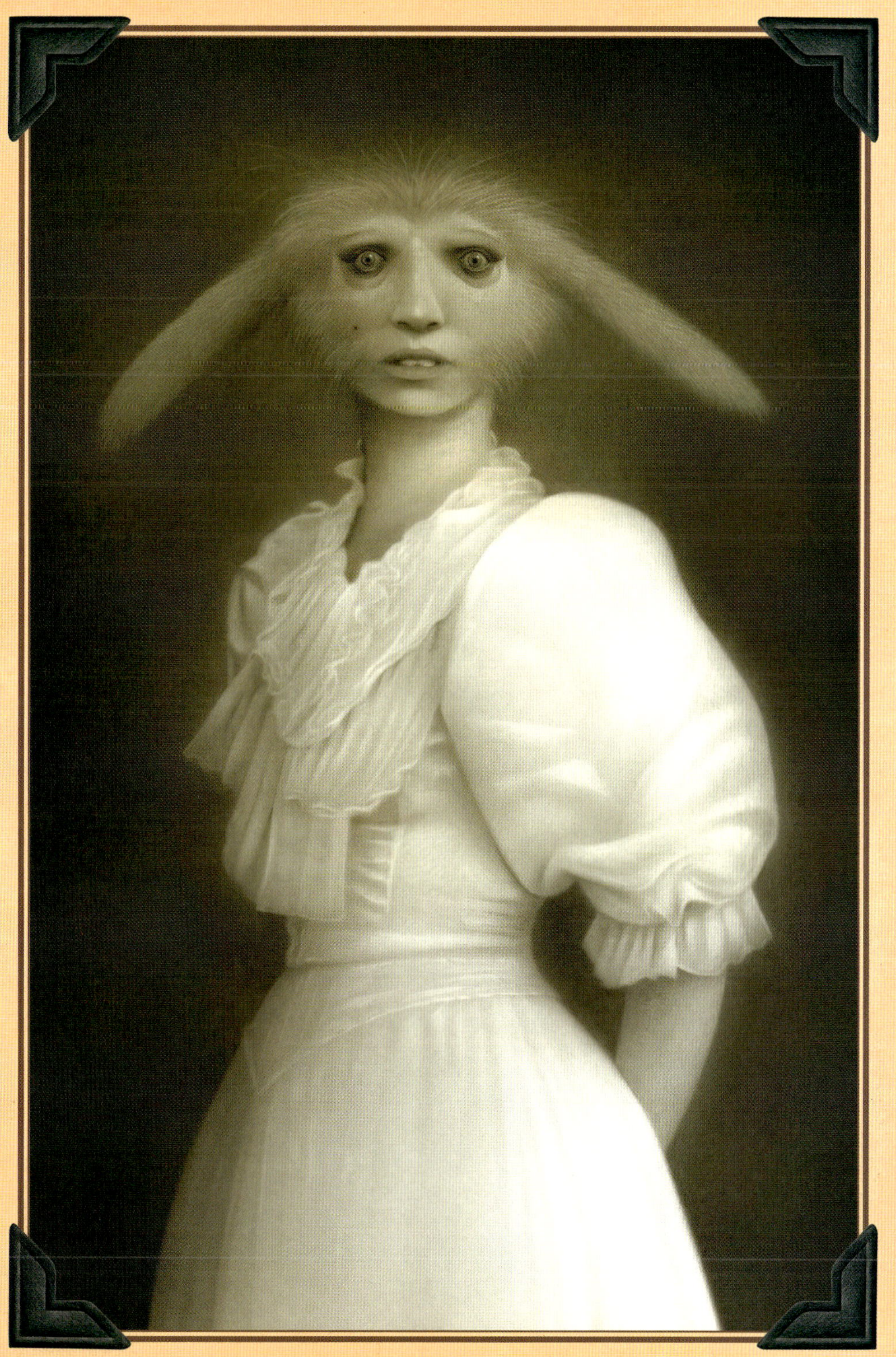

MISS BUNNY

Naven's anxiety about spiders began when he was a small boy, in Yorkshire. While helping his father with some masonry work at the local church, he was bitten by a brown spider just at the top of his head. As a result, he lost the pigmentation in his eyes along with most of the hair surrounding the bite, which did not grow back. He spent the rest of his youth wearing hats, answering questions about his unusual circumstances and, of course, avoiding spiders.

After years of being teased, (children can be so cruel) and explaining the premature baldness, he forced himself to overcome his spider phobia by venturing into his father's spider-filled cellar and allowing the arachnids to crawl on his head. He grew to admire these long-legged creatures and began keeping them as pets, eventually becoming a celebrated spider collector and enthusiast.

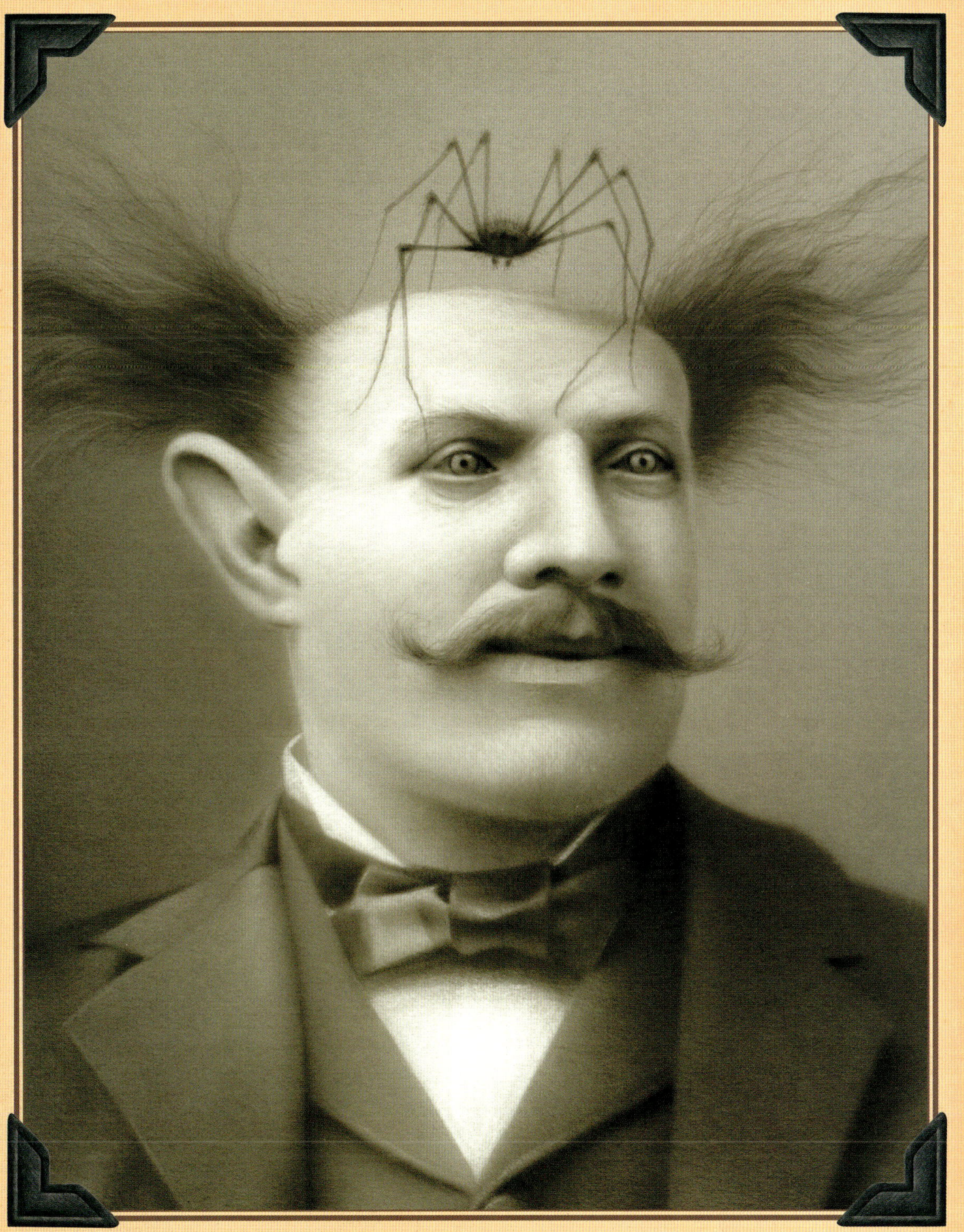

NAVEN OVERCOMES HIS SPIDER PHOBIA

In 1873, a young sheep herder in the North Yorkshire Moors made a startling discovery. He found what appeared to be a man buried vertically in the ground. Only his head was underneath the soil, and he was balanced with feet and hands completely off the ground and stretched toward the sunlight like the branches of a tree. The boy quickly thought to pull the man out of the ground to "save" him from suffocating. There was so much resistance he had to use a team of draft horses to unearth the man, whose arms and legs were flailing and kicking about. Once the man was freed from the soil, the boy was astonished to see what appeared to be roots protruding from the man's misshapen head. The root-headed man quickly ran off and disappeared into the foggy Moors.

He reappeared some twenty-five years later in North America. He was part of a traveling sideshow where he was billed as the "Curious Ginseng Man." It was said that spending time in his presence was invigorating, but too much time spent with him caused bouts of extreme insomnia.

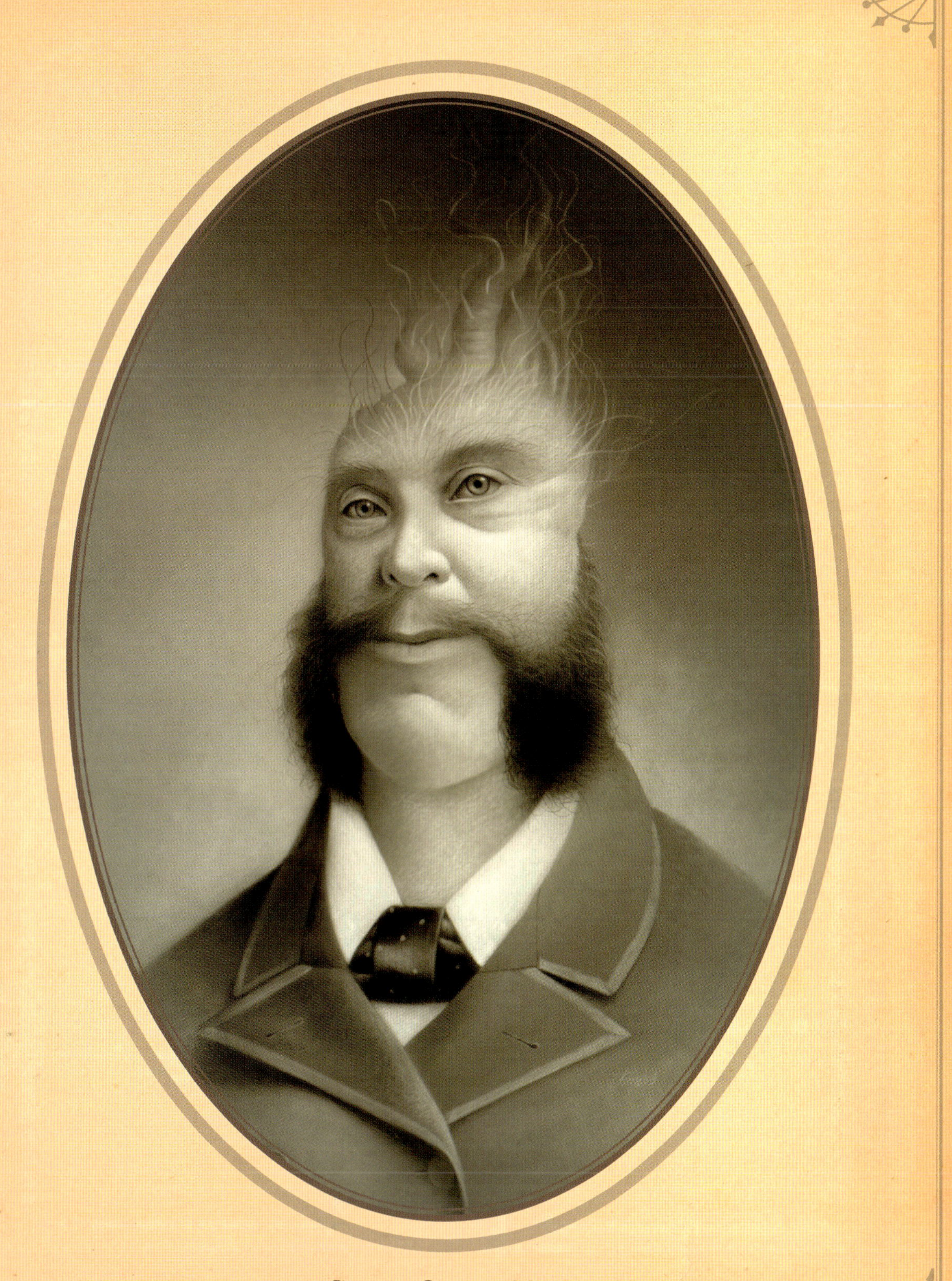

CURIOUS GINSENG MAN

If you paid close attention to the sixth step in an old Victorian household, you might notice a set of eyes staring back out at you from behind the stairs. That was Thurston. He traveled from house to house living under the stairs. He had a fondness for little people. (Little people were commonly found in Victorian country homes where they caused minor mischief or made shoes.) Thurston often came out from under the stairs to play with the little people.

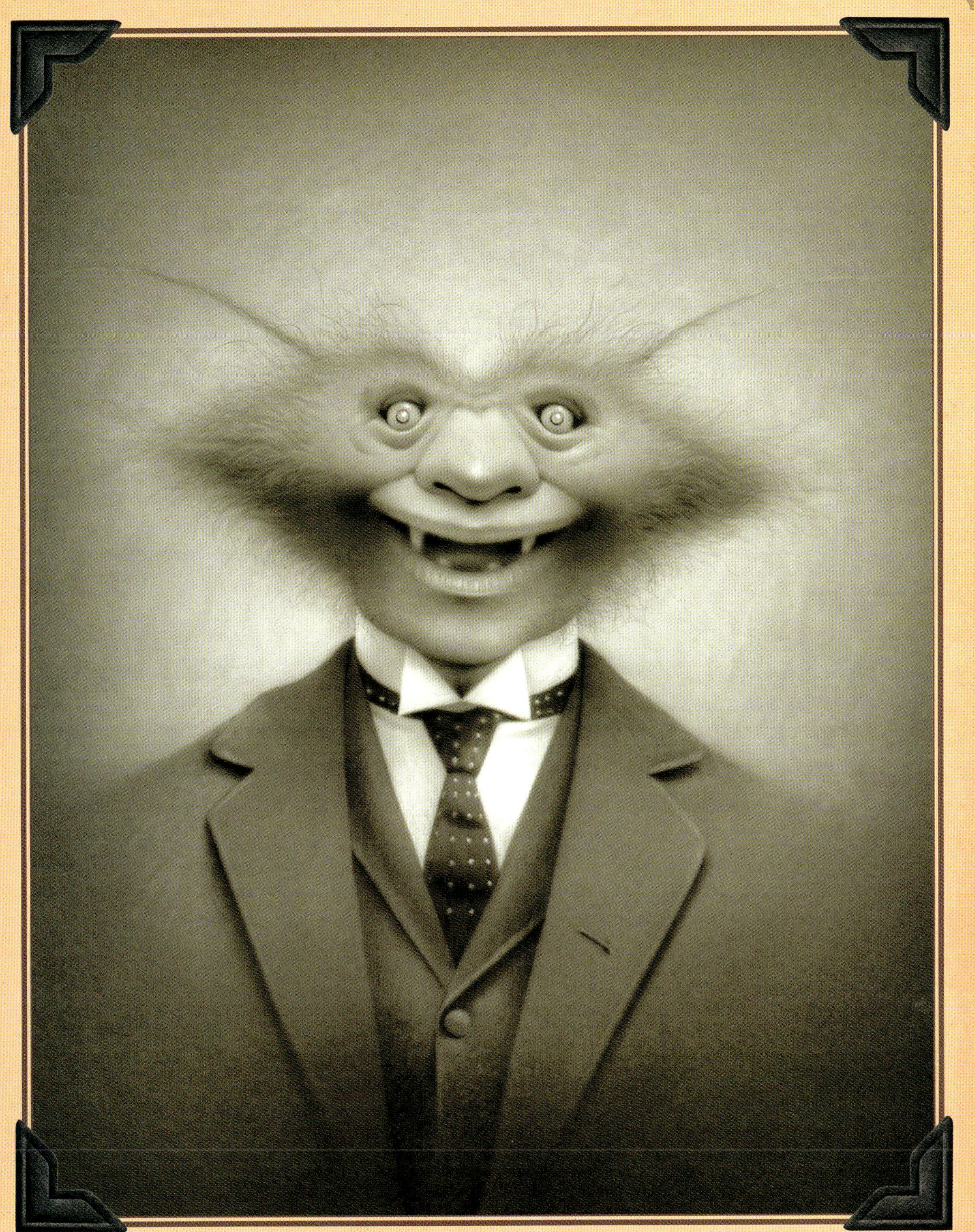

THURSTON FROM UNDER THE STAIRS

NORMAN LIVED IN A SMALL COTTAGE OUTSIDE OF LONDON THAT HE SHARED
with his pet weta, Jenkins, (a large cricket-like insect, native to islands in
and around New Zealand). Unlike ordinary insects, Jenkins had the ability
to control people's minds. Did he use that ability for good or evil? No one
knew for certain, but Norman lived happily with his "pet." He did find it
curious that the local townspeople often addressed him as "King Norman"
or "Your Majesty," and when the town tax collector arrived at his home to
make an assessment, the collector cried out that his eyes were on fire and
jumped into the pond.

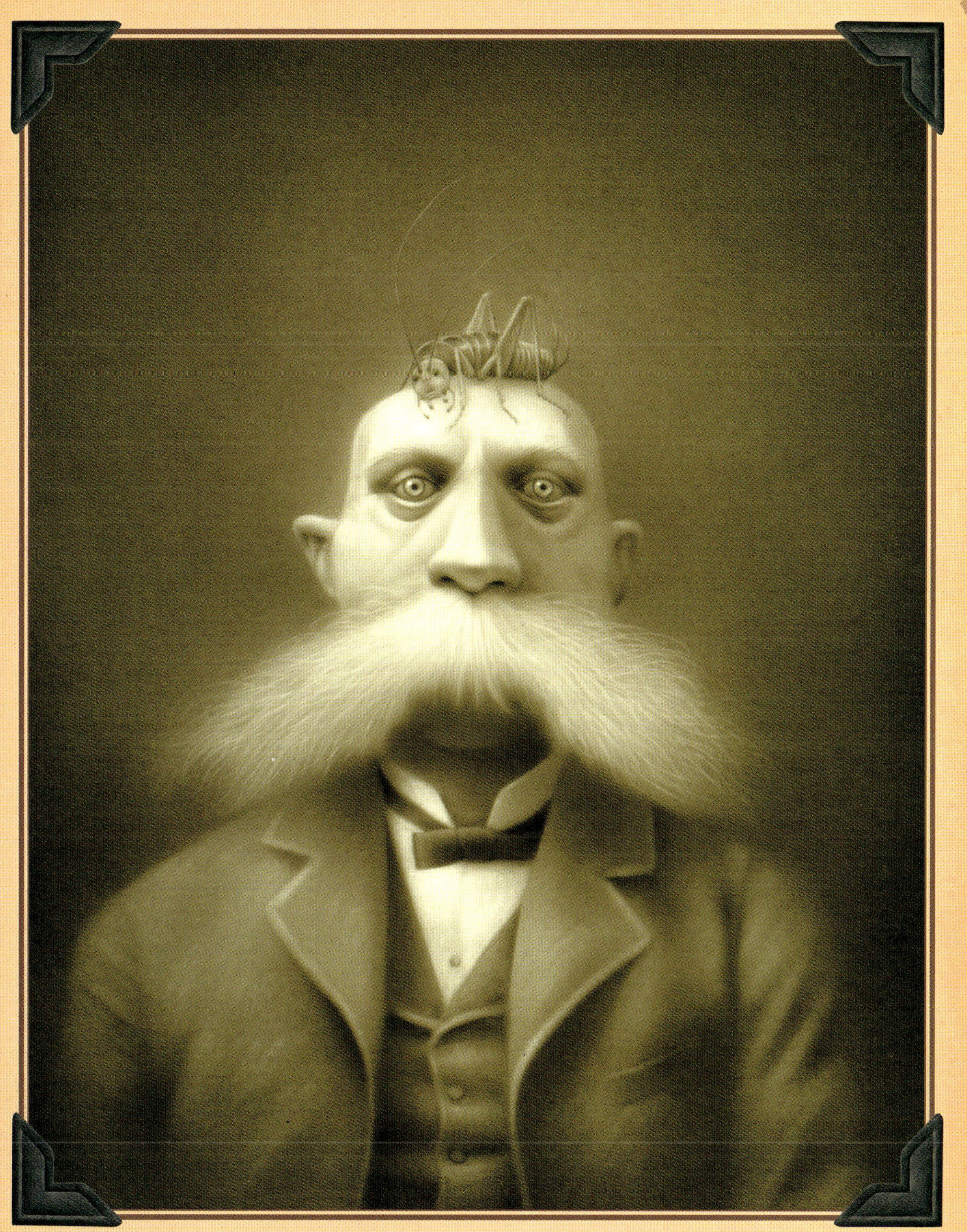

NORMAN AND JENKINS

MOLLY WAS BLAMED FOR MOST OF THE BAD HAIR IN WALES. IN 1897, SHE WAS forced to leave her town and went on a steam ship bound for New York. When the boat reached the harbor, all the passengers on board had acquired her "bad hair."

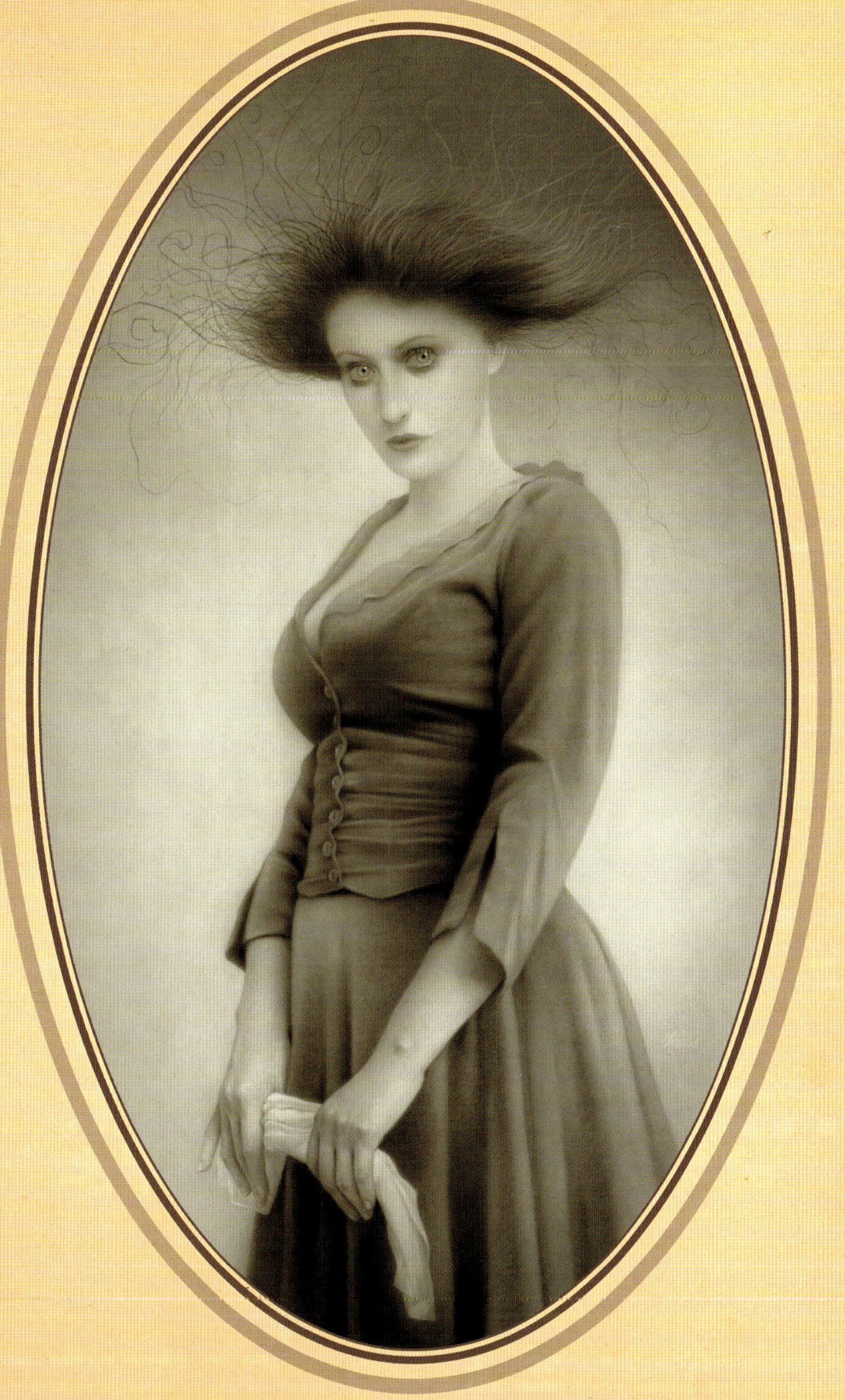

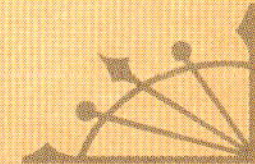

⊷ Molly Bad Hair ⊶

WHILE POSING FOR A FORMAL PORTRAIT, YOUNG MISS BUNNY HAD A SAD FEELING when her hands touched some rabbit fur. She had always wondered what had happened to her family. She never found out that they were devoured by wild dogs. At a young age she was discovered wandering the woods outside Hastings, was adopted by a wealthy London family, and lived what many would consider a charmed life.

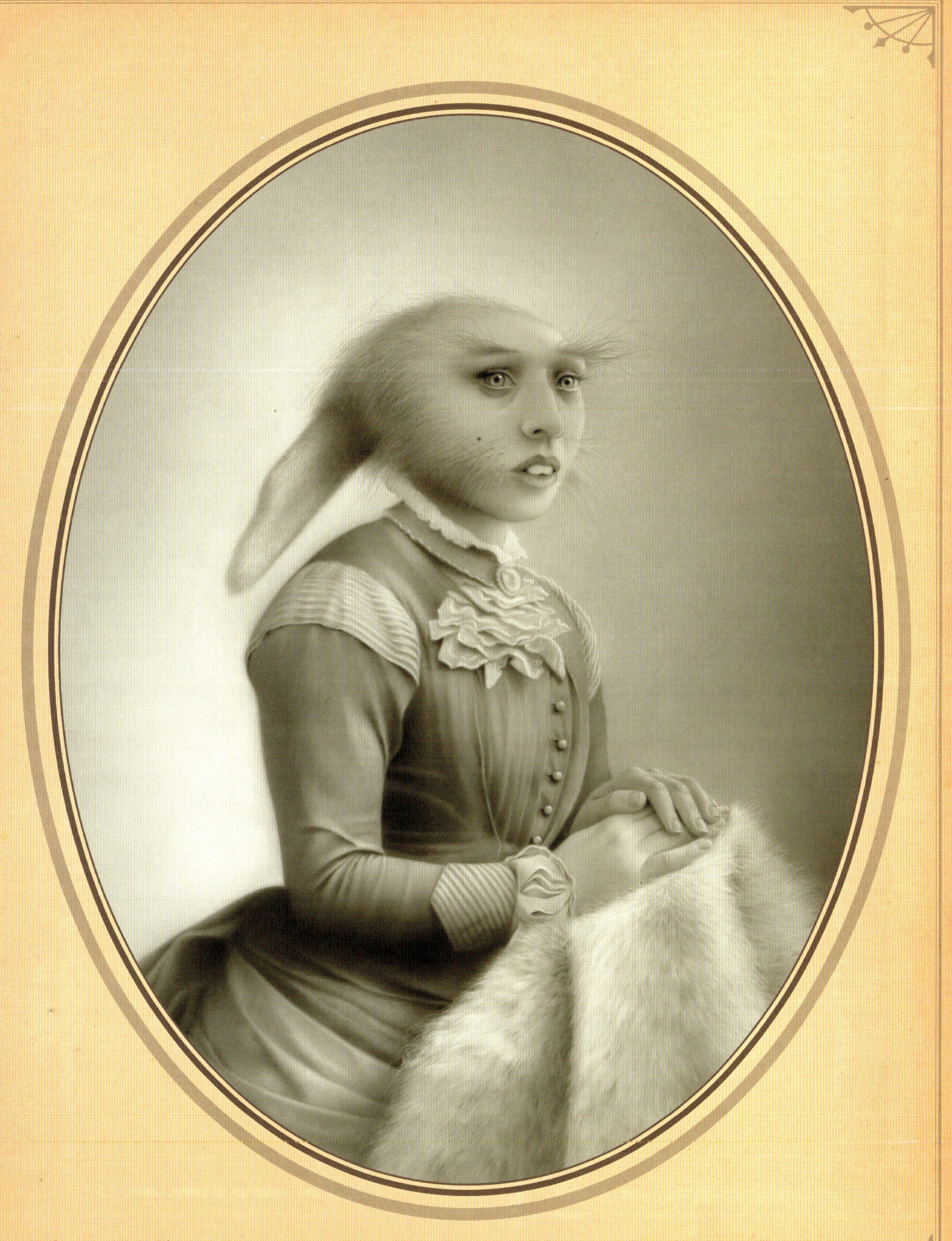

Young Miss Bunny

Sally was a very large and very mean ogre. When she grew tired of terrorizing the English countryside, she was hired as an enforcer on board a pirate ship. Pirating was a short-lived occupation and at the turn of the 19th century she decided to settle in Sheffield where she invested all her stolen treasures in the steel industry. At 150 years old, she was the typical middle-aged ogre; her vision was starting to go and her lower back pain was becoming intolerable. She took her earnings and bought property in New York and rented office space in Lower Manhattan.

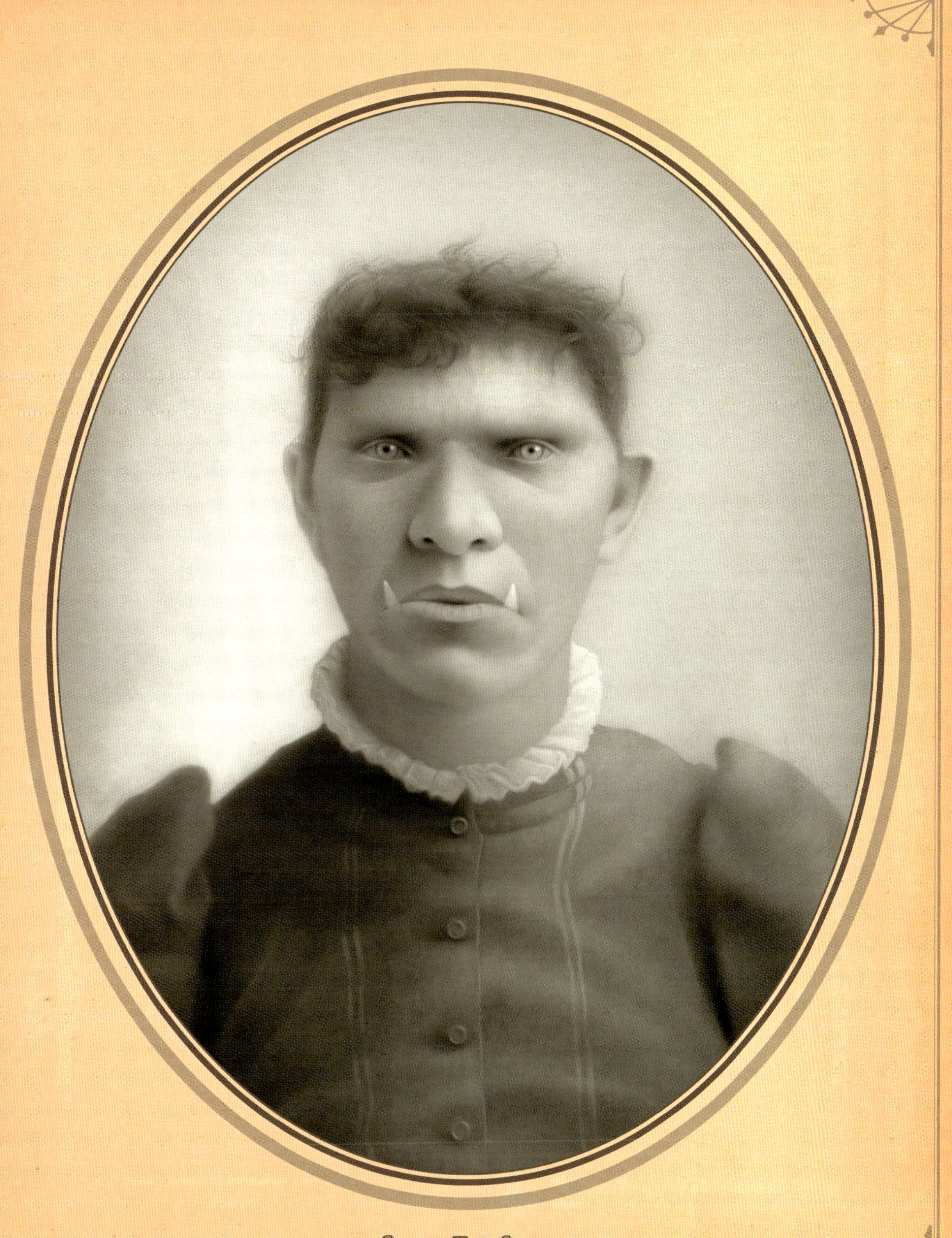

SALLY THE GOON

I'd like to thank Bob Self and Jensen Karp for making this book possible.

Special thanks to Kirsten Anderson for believing in my work in the first place and continuing to encourage my growth as an artist.

I'd like to thank all the art galleries, art dealers, and collectors who have supported me: Roq La Rue Gallery, The Shooting Gallery, Joshua Liner Gallery, Copro Nason Gallery, Merry Karnowsky Gallery, Gallery 1988, Yves Laroche Galerie d'art, Fuse Gallery, Gary Pressman, Justin Giarla and Kirsten, Merry Karnowsky, Jamie O'Shea, Joshua Liner, Greg Escalante, Gregory Teodori, Billy Shire, Annie Adjchavanich, Yves Laroche, Paul Booth, LC, Brad Keech, Jay Nailor, Les Claypool, Brad Benedict, Katie Cromwell, Jan Corey, Bruce Helford, Erik Foss, Guillermo del Toro (not only for his support, but also for allowing us to view his fantastic, imaginary world), Matthew Gold, Glenn Bray, Chris Ward, Jeff Wardell, Monte Beauchamp, Mark Parker, Morgan Spurlock, Adrian Grenier, Hung-Hei Yung, Robert O'Brien, Jim and Tara Kruse, Jon Alagem, Spencer Smith, Aristides & Heather Pinedo-Burns, Gino Joukar, Jenny Mollen and Jason Biggs . . .

I'd also like to thank some of my friends and fellow artists for their inspiration: Diana Louie (for being my best friend, best cheerleader, time manager, and psychoanalyst), Paul Ranieri (for sticking by me all these years and backing me up in uncertain times), Mark Elliott (for always reminding me what is within the realm of possibility), Kato DeStefan, Chet Zar, Robert Hardgrave, Molly Crabapple, Fred Harper, Mark Murphy, Kathie Olivas, Brandt Peters, Colin & Sas Christian, Lola, Greg Simkins, Joe Capobianco, Stephen Hickman, Dave Chung, Chris Ryniak, Kris Lewis, Ron English, Nathan Spoor, Peter Gong, Stewart Goldstein, Stephen Price, Kirk Reinert, Mark Garro, Jason D'Aquino, Amber Tamblyn, Van Arno, Robert Craig, Anthony Pontius, Femke Hiemstra, Angie Mason, Attaboy, Annie Owens, KuKula, Audrey Kawasaki, Amy Sol, Mario "MARS-1" Martinez, Miles Teves, Martin Wittfooth, Bill Basso, Todd & Kathy Schorr, Isabel Samaras, Heiko Müeller, Mike Leavitt, Adam Wallacavage, Zoetica Ebb, Robert Williams, Luke Chueh, Joshua Petker, Shawn Barber, Brendan Danielsson, Chris Mostyn, Chris Conte, Lori Earley, Matthew Bone, Jasmine Worth, Carrie Ann Baade, Lily Feliciano, Tony Romel, Vince Natale, Laurie Young, Bill Fold, Mark Frauenfelder, Yul Brynner, Steve McQueen, James Coburn, Horst Buchholz, Brad Dexter, Charles Bronson, Robert Vaughn and Eli Wallach.

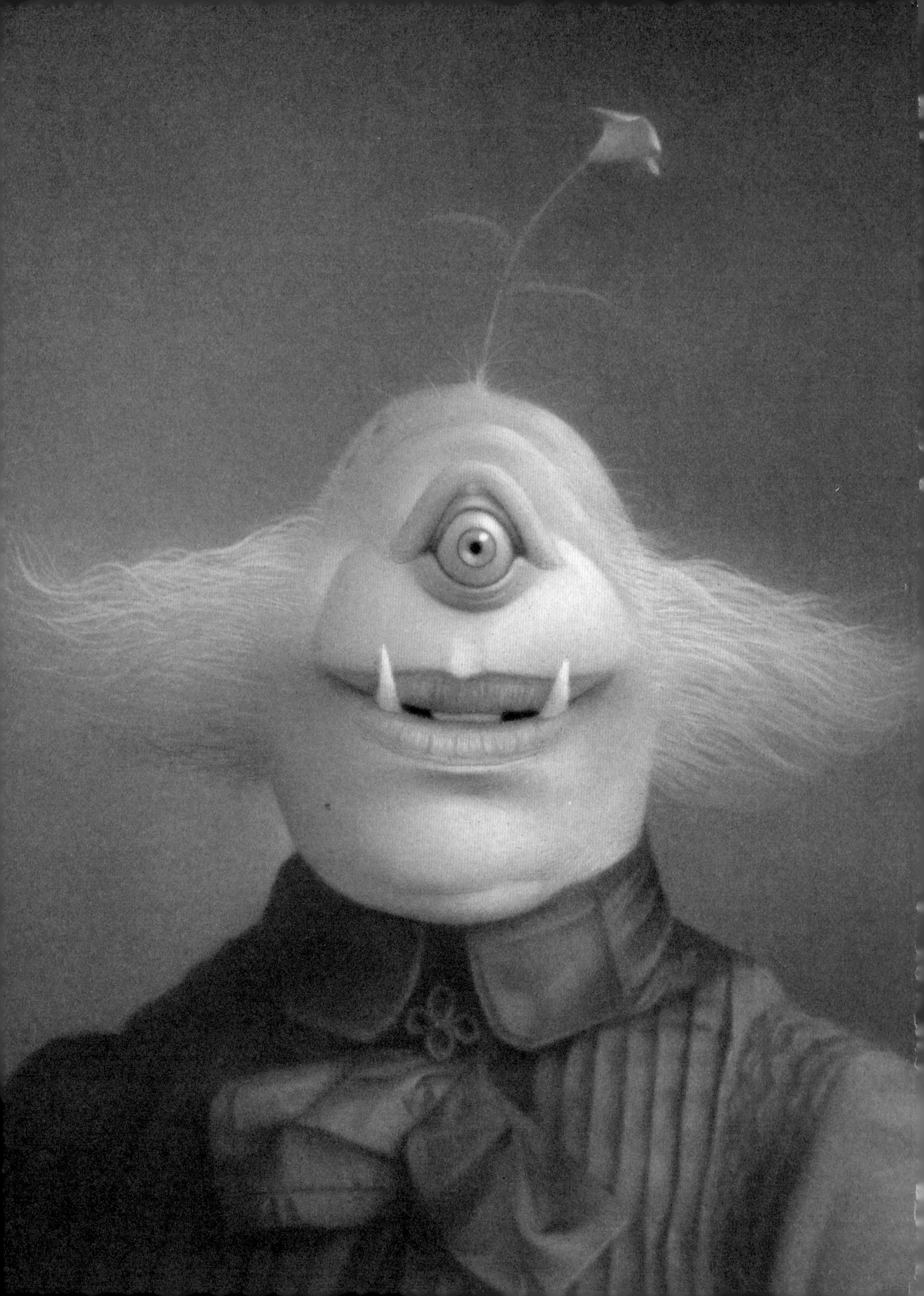